The Plymouth Express Affair

& OTHER STORIES

Agatha Christie

Pharos Books

ISBN: 978-93-55465-83-2
eISBN: 978-93-55465-84-9

©Publisher

Publisher: Pharos Books (P) Ltd.
Plot No.-55, Main Mother Dairy Road
Pandav Nagar, East Delhi-110092
Phone: 011-40395855, +4049916623
WhatsApp: +91 8368220032
E-mail: sales@pharosbooks.in
Website: www.pharosbooks.in
First Edition: 2023

Printed By: Sushma Book Binding House, Okhla
Industrial Area, Phase II, New Delhi-110020

The Plymouth Express Affair & Other Stories
By Agatha Christie

CONTENTS

The Plymouth Express Affair

Alec Simpson, R. N., stepped from the platform at Newton Abbot into a first-class compartment of the Plymouth Express. A porter followed him with a heavy suitcase. He was about to swing it up to the rack, but the young sailor stopped him.

"No—leave it on the seat. I'll put it up later. Here you are."

"Thank you, sir." The porter, generously tipped, withdrew.

Doors banged; a stentorian voice shouted: "Plymouth only. Change for Torquay. Plymouth next stop." Then a whistle blew, and the train drew slowly out of the station.

Lieutenant Simpson had the carriage to himself. The December air was chilly, and he pulled up the window. Then he sniffed vaguely, and frowned. What a smell there was! Reminded him of that time in hospital, and the operation on his leg. Yes, chloroform; that was it!

He let the window down again, changing his seat to one with its back to the engine. He pulled a pipe out of his pocket and lit it. For a little time he sat inactive, looking out into the night and smoking.

At last he roused himself, and opening the suitcase, took out some papers and magazines, then closed the suitcase again and endeavored to shove it under the opposite seat—without success. Some hidden obstacle resisted it. He shoved harder with rising impatience, but it still stuck out halfway into the carriage.

"Why the devil wont it go in?" he muttered, and hauling it out completely, he stooped down and peered under the seat....

A moment later a cry rang out into the night, and the great train came to an unwilling halt in obedience to the imperative jerking of the communication-cord.

"Mon ami," said Poirot. "You have, I know, been deeply interested in this mystery of the Plymouth Express. Read this."

I picked up the note he flicked across the table to me. It was brief and to the point.

Dear Sir:

I shall be obliged if you will call upon me at your earliest convenience.

Yours faithfully,
EBENEZER HALLIDAY.

The connection was not clear to my mind, and I looked inquiringly at Poirot. For answer he took up the newspaper and read aloud:

"'A sensational discovery was made last night. A young naval officer returning to Plymouth found under the seat of his compartment, the body of a woman, stabbed through the heart. The officer at once pulled the communication-cord, and the train was brought to a standstill. The woman who was about thirty years of age, and richly dressed, has not yet been identified.'

"And later we have this: 'The woman found dead in the Plymouth Express has been identified as the Honorable Mrs. Rupert Carrington.' You see now, my friend? Or if you do not, I will add this. Mrs. Rupert Carrington was, before her marriage, Flossie Halliday, daughter of old man Halliday, the steel king of America."

"And he has sent for you? Splendid!"

"I did him a little service in the past—an affair of bearer bonds. And once, when I was in Paris for a royal visit, I had Mademoiselle Flossie pointed out to me. *La jolie petite pensionnaire!* She had the *jolie dot* too! It caused trouble. She nearly made a bad affair."

"How was that?"

                    The Plymouth Express Affair & Other Stories

"A certain Count de la Rochefour. *Un bien mauvais sujet!* A bad hat, as you would say. An adventurer pure and simple, who knew how to appeal to a romantic young girl. Luckily her father got wind of it in time. He took her back to America in haste. I heard of her marriage some years later, but I know nothing of her husband."

"H'm," I said. "The Honorable Rupert Carrington is no beauty, by all accounts. He'd pretty well run through his own money on the turf, and I should imagine old man Halliday's dollars came along in the nick of time. I should say that for a good-looking, well-mannered, utterly unscrupulous young scoundrel, it would be hard to find his match!"

"Ah, the poor little lady! *Elle n'est pas bien tombée!*"

"I fancy he made it pretty obvious at once that it was her money, and not she, that had attracted him. I believe they drifted apart almost at once. I have heard rumors lately that there was to be a definite legal separation."

"Old man Halliday is no fool. He would tie up her money pretty tight."

"I dare say. Anyway, I know as a fact that the Honorable Rupert is said to be extremely hard up."

"Ah-ha! I wonder—"

"You wonder what?"

"My good friend, do not jump down my throat like that. You are interested, I see. Supposing you accompany me to see Mr. Halliday. There is a taxi stand at the corner."

A very few minutes sufficed to whirl us to the superb house in Park Lane rented by the American magnate. We were shown into the library, and almost immediately we were joined by a large, stout man, with piercing eyes and an aggressive chin.

"M. Poirot?" said Mr. Halliday. "I guess I don't need to tell you what I want you for. You've read the papers, and I'm never one to let the grass grow under my feet. I happened to hear you were in London, and I remembered the good work you did over those bonds. Never forget a name. I've got the pick of Scotland Yard, but I'll have my own man as well. Money no object. All the dollars were made for my little girl—and now she's gone, I'll spend my last cent to catch the damned scoundrel that did it! See? So it's up to you to deliver the goods."

Poirot bowed.

"I accept, monsieur, all the more willingly that I saw your daughter in Paris several times. And now I will ask you to tell me the circumstances of her journey to Plymouth and any other details that seem to you to bear upon the case."

"Well, to begin with," responded Halliday, "she wasn't going to Plymouth. She was going to join a house-party at Avonmead Court, the Duchess of Swansea's place. She left London by the twelve-fourteen from Paddington, arriving at Bristol (where she had to change) at two-fifty. The principal Plymouth expresses, of course, run via Westbury, and do not go near Bristol at all. The twelve-fourteen does a nonstop run to Bristol, afterward stopping at Weston, Taunton, Exeter and Newton Abbot. My daughter traveled alone in her carriage, which was reserved as far as Bristol, her maid being in a third-class carriage in the next coach."

Poirot nodded, and Mr. Halliday went on: "The party at Avonmead Court was to be a very gay one, with several balls, and in consequence my daughter had with her nearly all her jewels—amounting in value perhaps, to about a hundred thousand dollars."

"*Un moment*," interrupted Poirot. "Who had charge of the jewels? Your daughter, or the maid?"

"My daughter always took charge of them herself, carrying them in a small blue morocco case."

"Continue, monsieur."

"At Bristol the maid, Jane Mason, collected her mistress' dressing-bag and wraps, which were with her, and came to the door of Flossie's compartment. To her intense surprise, my daughter told her that she was not getting out at Bristol, but was going on farther. She directed Mason to get out the luggage and put it in the cloak-room. She could have tea in the refreshment-room, but she was to wait at the station for her mistress, who would return to Bristol by an up-train in the course of the afternoon. The maid, although very much astonished, did as she was told. She put the luggage in the cloak-room and had some tea. But up-train after up-train came in, and her mistress did not appear. After the arrival of the last train, she left the luggage where it was, and went to a hotel near the station for the night. This morning she read of the tragedy, and returned to town by the first available train."

"Is there nothing to account for your daughter's sudden change of plan?"

"Well, there is this: According to Jane Mason, at Bristol, Flossie was no longer alone in her carriage. There was a man in it who stood looking out of the farther window so that she could not see his face."

"The train was a corridor one, of course?"

"Yes."

"Which side was the corridor?"

"On the platform side. My daughter was standing in the corridor as she talked to Mason."

"And there is no doubt in your mind—excuse me!" He got up, and carefully straightened the inkstand which was a little askew. "*Je vous demande pardon*," he continued, reseating himself. "It affects my nerves to see anything crooked. Strange, is it not? I was saying, monsieur, that there is no doubt in your mind, as to this probably unexpected meeting being the cause of your daughter's sudden change of plan?"

"It seems the only reasonable supposition."

"You have no idea as to who the gentleman in question might be?"

The millionaire hesitated for a moment, and then replied.

"No—I do not know at all."

"Now—as to the discovery of the body?"

"It was discovered by a young naval officer who at once gave the alarm. There was a doctor on the train. He examined the body. She had been first chloroformed, and then stabbed. He gave it as his opinion that she had been dead about four hours, so it must have been done not long after leaving Bristol. —Probably between there and Weston, possibly between Weston and Taunton."

"And the jewel-case."

"The jewel-case, M. Poirot, was missing."

"One thing more, monsieur. Your daughter's fortune—to whom does it pass at her death?"

"Flossie made a will soon after her marriage, leaving everything to her husband." He hesitated for a minute, and then went on: "I may as well tell you, Monsieur Poirot, that I regard my son-in-law as an unprincipled scoundrel, and that, by my advice, my daughter was on the eve of freeing herself from him by legal means—no difficult matter. I settled her money upon her in such a way that he could not touch it during her lifetime, but although they have lived entirely apart for some years, she has frequently acceded to his demands for money, rather than face an open scandal. However, I was determined to put an end to this, and at last Flossie agreed, and my lawyers were instructed to take proceedings."

"And where is Monsieur Carrington?"

"In town. I believe he was away in the country yesterday, but he returned last night."

Poirot considered a little while. Then he said: "I think that is all, monsieur."

"You would like to see the maid, Jane Mason?"

"If you please."

Halliday rang the bell, and gave a short order to the footman. A few minutes later Jane Mason entered the room, a respectable, hard-featured woman, as emotionless in the face of tragedy as only a good servant can be.

"You will permit me to put a few questions? Your mistress, she was quite as usual before starting yesterday morning? Not excited or flurried?"

"Oh, no sir!"

"But at Bristol she was quite different?"

"Yes sir, regular upset—so nervous she didn't seem to know what she was saying."

"What did she say exactly?"

"Well sir, as near as I can remember, she said: 'Mason, I've got to alter my plans. Something has happened—I mean, I'm not getting out here after all. I must go on. Get out the luggage and put it in the cloak-room; then have some tea, and wait for me in the station.'

"'Wait for you here, ma'am?' I asked.

"'Yes, yes. Don't leave the station. I shall return by a later train. I don't know when. It mayn't be until quite late.'

"'Very well, ma'am,' I says. It wasn't my place to ask questions, but I thought it very strange."

"It was unlike your mistress, eh?"

"Very unlike her, sir."

"What did you think?"

"Well sir, I thought it was to do with the gentleman in the carriage. She didn't speak to him, but she turned round once or twice as though to ask him if she was doing right."

"But you didn't see the gentleman's face?"

"No sir; he stood with his back to me all the time."

"Can you describe him at all?"

"He had on a light fawn overcoat, and a traveling cap. He was tall and slender, like, and the back of his head was dark."

"You didn't know him?"

"Oh, no, I don't think so, sir."

"It was not your master, Mr. Carrington, by any chance?"

Mason looked rather startled.

"Oh! I don't think so, sir!"

"But you are not *sure*?"

"It was about the master's build, sir—but I never thought of it being him. We so seldom saw him. I couldn't say it *wasn't* him!"

Poirot picked up a pin from the carpet, and frowned at it severely; then he continued: "Would it be possible for the man to have entered the train at Bristol before you reached the carriage?"

Mason considered.

"Yes sir, I think it would. My compartment was very crowded, and it was some minutes before I could get out—and then there was a very large crowd on the platform, and that delayed me too. But he'd only have had a minute or two to speak to the mistress, that way. I took it for granted that he'd come along the corridor."

"That is more probable, certainly."

He paused, still frowning.

"You know how the mistress was dressed, sir?"

"The papers give a few details, but I would like you to confirm them."

"She was wearing a white fox fur toque, sir, with a white spotted veil, and a blue frieze coat and skirt—the shade of blue they call electric."

"H'm, rather striking."

"Yes," remarked Halliday. "Inspector Japp is in hopes that that may help us to fix the spot where the crime took place. Anyone who saw her would remember her."

"*Précisément!* —Thank you, mademoiselle." The maid left the room.

"Well!" Poirot got up briskly. "That is all I can do here—except, monsieur, that I would ask you to tell me everything—but *everything*!"

"I have done so."

"You are sure?"

"Absolutely."

"Then there is nothing more to be said. I must decline the case."

"Why?"

"Because you have not been frank with me."

"I assure you—"

"No, you are keeping something back."

There was a moment's pause, and then Halliday drew a paper from his pocket and handed it to my friend.

"I guess that's what you're after, Monsieur Poirot—though how you know about it fairly gets my goat!"

Poirot smiled, and unfolded the paper. It was a letter written in thin sloping handwriting. Poirot read it aloud.

"'Chère Madame:

"'It is with infinite pleasure that I look forward to the felicity of meeting you again. After your so amiable reply to my letter, I can hardly restrain my impatience. I have never forgotten those days in Paris. It is most cruel that you should be leaving London tomorrow. However, before very long, and perhaps sooner than you think, I shall have the joy of beholding once more the lady whose image has ever reigned supreme in my heart.

"'Believe, chère madame, all the assurances of my most devoted and unaltered sentiments—

"'Armand de la Rochefour.'"

Poirot handed the letter back to Halliday with a bow.

"I fancy, monsieur, that you did not know that your daughter intended renewing her acquaintance with the Count de la Rochefour?"

"It came as a thunderbolt to me! I found this letter in my daughter's handbag. As you probably know, Monsieur Poirot, this so-called count is an adventurer of the worst type."

Poirot nodded.

"But what I want to know is how you knew of the existence of this letter?"

My friend smiled. "Monsieur, I did not. But to track footmarks, and recognize cigarette-ash is not sufficient for a detective. He must also be a good psychologist! I knew that you disliked and mistrusted your son-in-law. He benefits by your daughter's death; the maid's description of the mysterious man bears a sufficient resemblance to him. Yet you are not keen on his track! Why? Surely because your suspicions lie in another direction. Therefore you were keeping something back."

"You're right, Monsieur Poirot. I was sure of Rupert's guilt until I found this letter. It unsettled me horribly."

"Yes. The Count says: 'Before very long, and perhaps sooner than you think.' Obviously he would not want to wait until you should get wind of his reappearance. Was it he who traveled down from London by the twelve-fourteen, and came along the corridor to your daughter's compartment? The Count de la Rochefour is also, if I remember rightly, tall and dark!"

The millionaire nodded.

"Well, monsieur, I will wish you good day. Scotland Yard, has, I presume, a list of the jewels?"

"Yes, I believe Inspector Japp is here now if you would like to see him."

Japp was an old friend of ours, and greeted Poirot with a sort of affectionate contempt.

"And how are you, monsieur? No bad feeling between us, though we *have* got our different ways of looking at things. How are the 'little gray cells,' eh? Going strong?"

Poirot beamed upon him. "They function, my good Japp; assuredly they do!"

"Then that's all right. Think it was the Honorable Rupert, or a crook? We're keeping an eye on all the regular places, of course. We shall know if the shiners are disposed of, and of course whoever did it isn't going to keep them to admire their sparkle. Not likely! I'm trying to find out where Rupert Carrington was yesterday. Seems a bit of a mystery about it. I've got a man watching him."

"A great precaution, but perhaps a day late," suggested Poirot gently.

"You always will have your joke, Monsieur Poirot. Well, I'm off to Paddington. Bristol, Weston, Taunton, that's my beat. So long."

"You will come round and see me this evening, and tell me the result?"

"Sure thing, if I'm back."

"That good Inspector believes in matter in motion," murmured Poirot as our friend departed. "He travels; he measures footprints; he collects mud and cigarette-ash! He is extremely busy! He is zealous beyond words! And if I mentioned psychology to him, do you know what he would do, my friend? He would smile! He would say to himself: 'Poor old Poirot! He ages! He grows senile!' Japp is the 'younger generation knocking on the door.' And *ma foi!* They are so busy knocking that they do not notice that the door is open!"

"And what are you going to do?"

"As we have *carte blanche,* I shall expend threepence in ringing up the Ritz—where you may have noticed our Count is staying. After that, as my feet are a little damp, and I have sneezed twice, I shall return to my rooms and make myself a *tisano* over the spirit lamp!"

I did not see Poirot again until the following morning. I found him placidly finishing his breakfast.

"Well?" I inquired eagerly. "What has happened?"

"Nothing."

"But Japp?"

"I have not seen him."

"The Count?"

"He left the Ritz the day before yesterday."

"The day of the murder?"

"Yes."

"Then that settles it! Rupert Carrington is cleared."

"Because the Count de la Rochefour has left the Ritz? You go too fast, my friend."

"Anyway, he must be followed, arrested! But what could be his motive?"

"One hundred thousand dollars' worth of jewelry is a very good motive for anyone. No, the question to my mind is: why kill her? Why not simply steal the jewels? She would not prosecute."

"Why not?"

"Because she is a woman, *mon ami*. She once loved this man. Therefore she would suffer her loss in silence. And the Count, who is an extremely good psychologist where women are concerned,—hence his successes,—would know that perfectly well! On the other hand, if Rupert Carrington killed her, why take the jewels, which would incriminate him fatally?"

"As a blind."

"Perhaps you are right, my friend. Ah, here is Japp! I recognize his knock."

    The Plymouth Express Affair & Other Stories

The Inspector was beaming good-humoredly.

"Morning, Poirot. Only just got back. I've done some good work! And you?"

"Me, I have arranged my ideas," replied Poirot placidly.

Japp laughed heartily.

"Old chap's getting on in years," he observed beneath his breath to me. "That wont do for us young folk," he said aloud.

"*Quel dommage?*" Poirot inquired.

"Well, do you want to hear what I've done?"

"You permit me to make a guess? You have found the knife with which the crime was committed by the side of the line between Weston and Taunton, and you have interviewed the paper-boy who spoke to Mrs. Carrington at Weston!"

Japp's jaw fell. "How on earth did you know? Don't tell me it was those almighty 'little gray cells' of yours!"

"I am glad you admit for once that they are *all mighty*! Tell me, did she give the paper-boy a shilling for himself?"

"No, it was half a crown!" Japp recovered his temper and grinned. "Pretty extravagant, these rich Americans!"

"And in consequence the boy did not forget her?"

"Not he. Half-crowns don't come his way every day. She hailed him and bought two magazines. One had a picture of a girl in blue on the cover. 'That'll match me,' she said. Oh! he remembered her perfectly. Well, that was enough for me. By the doctor's evidence, the crime *must* have been committed before Taunton. I guessed they'd throw the knife away at once, and I walked down the line looking for it; and sure enough, there it was. I made inquiries at Taunton about our man, but of course it's a big station, and it wasn't likely they'd notice him. He probably got back to London by a later train."

Poirot nodded. "Very likely."

"But I found another bit of news when I got back. They're passing the jewels, all right! That large emerald was pawned last night—by one of the regular lot. Who do you think it was?"

"I don't know—except that he was a short man."

Japp stared. "Well, you're right there. He's short enough. It was Red Narky."

"Who on earth is Red Narky?" I asked.

"A particularly sharp jewel-thief, sir. And not one to stick at murder. Usually works with a woman—Gracie Kidd; but she doesn't seem to be in it this time—unless she's got off to Holland with the rest of the swag."

"You've arrested Narky?"

"Sure thing. But mind you, it's the other man we want—the man who went down with Mrs. Carrington in the train. He was the one who planned the job, right enough. But Narky wont squeal on a pal."

I noticed that Poirot's eyes had become very green.

"I think," he said gently, "that I can find Narky's pal for you, all right."

"One of your little ideas, eh?" Japp eyed Poirot sharply. "Wonderful how you manage to deliver the goods sometimes, at your age and all. Devil's own luck, of course."

"Perhaps, perhaps," murmured my friend. "Hastings, my hat. And the brush. So! My galoshes if it still rains! We must not undo the good work of that *tisano*. Au revoir, Japp!"

"Good luck to you, Poirot."

Poirot hailed the first taxi we met, and directed the driver to Park Lane.

When we drew up before Halliday's house, he skipped out nimbly, paid the driver and rang the bell. To the footman who opened the door he made a request in a low voice, and we were immediately taken upstairs. We went up to the top of the house, and were shown into a small neat bedroom.

Poirot's eyes roved round the room and fastened themselves on a small black trunk. He knelt in front of it, scrutinized the labels on it, and took a small twist of wire from his pocket.

"Ask Mr. Halliday if he will be so kind as to mount to me here," he said over his shoulder to the footman.

(It is suggested that the reader pause in his perusal of the story at this point, make his own solution of the mystery—and then see how close he comes to that of the author.—The Editors.)

The man departed, and Poirot gently coaxed the lock of the trunk with a practiced hand. In a few minutes the lock gave, and he raised the lid of the trunk. Swiftly he began rummaging among the clothes it contained, flinging them out on the floor.

There was a heavy step on the stairs, and Halliday entered the room.

"What in hell are you doing here?" he demanded, staring.

"I was looking, monsieur, for *this*." Poirot withdrew from the trunk a coat and skirt of bright blue frieze, and a small toque of white fox fur.

"What are you doing with my trunk?" I turned to see that the maid, Jane Mason, had just entered the room.

"If you will just shut the door, Hastings. Thank you. Yes, and stand with your back against it. Now, Mr. Halliday, let me introduce you to Grace Kidd, otherwise Jane Mason, who will shortly rejoin her accomplice, Red Narky, under the kind escort of Japp."

"It was of the most simple." Poirot waved a deprecating hand, then helped himself to more caviare. It is not every day that one lunches with a millionaire.

"It was the maid's insistence on the clothes that her mistress was wearing that first struck me. Why was she so anxious that our attention should be directed to them? I reflected that we had only the maid's word for the mysterious man in the carriage at Bristol. As far as the doctor's evidence went, Mrs. Carrington might easily have been murdered *before* reaching Bristol. But if so, then the maid must be an accomplice. And if she were an accomplice, she would not wish this point to rest on her evidence alone. The clothes Mrs. Carrington was wearing were of a striking nature. A maid usually has a good deal of choice as to what her mistress shall wear. Now if, after Bristol, anyone saw a lady in a bright blue coat and skirt, and a fur toque, he will be quite ready to swear he has seen Mrs. Carrington.

"I began to reconstruct. The maid would provide herself with duplicate clothes. She and her accomplice chloroform and stab Mrs. Carrington between London and Bristol, probably taking advantage of a tunnel. Her body is rolled under the seat; the maid takes her place. At Weston she must make herself noticed. How? In all probability, a newspaper-boy will be selected. She will insure his remembering her by giving him a large tip. She also drew his attention to the color of her dress by a remark about one of the magazines. After leaving Weston, she throws the knife out of the window to mark the place where the crime presumably occurred, and changes her clothes, or buttons a long mackintosh over them. At Taunton she leaves the train and returns to Bristol as soon as possible, where her accomplice has duly left the luggage in the cloak-room. He hands over the ticket and himself returns to London. She waits on the platform, carrying out her rôle, goes to a hotel for the night and returns to town in the morning exactly as she said.

"When Japp returned from his expedition, he confirmed all my deductions. He also told me that a well-known crook was passing the jewels. I knew that whoever it was would be the exact opposite of the man Jane Mason described. When I heard that it was Red Narky, who always worked with Gracie Kidd—well, I knew just where to find her."

"And the Count?"

     The Plymouth Express Affair & Other Stories

"The more I thought of it, the more I was convinced that he had nothing to do with it. That gentleman is much too careful of his own skin to risk murder. It would be out of keeping with his character."

"Well, Monsieur Poirot," said Halliday. "I owe you a big debt. And the check I write after lunch wont go near to settling it."

Poirot smiled modestly, and murmured to me: "The good Japp, he shall get the official credit, all right, but though he has got his Gracie Kidd, I think that I, as the Americans say, have got his goat!"

Murder in the Mews

I

"Penny for the guy, sir?"

A small boy with a grimy face grinned ingratiatingly.

"Certainly not!" said Chief Inspector Japp. "And, look here, my lad—"

A short homily followed. The dismayed urchin beat a precipitate retreat, remarking briefly and succinctly to his youthful friends:

"Blimey, if it ain't a cop all togged up!"

The band took to its heels, chanting the incantation:

Remember, remember

The fifth of November

Gunpowder treason and plot.

We see no reason

Why gunpowder treason

Should ever be forgot.

The chief inspector's companion, a small, elderly man with an egg-shaped head and large, military-looking moustaches, was smiling to himself.

"Très bien, Japp," he observed. "You preach the sermon very well! I congratulate you!"

"Rank excuse for begging, that's what Guy Fawkes' Day is!" said Japp.

"An interesting survival," mused Hercule Poirot. "The fireworks go up—crack—crack—long after the man they commemorate and his deed are forgotten."

The Scotland Yard man agreed.

"Don't suppose many of those kids really know who Guy Fawkes was."

"And soon, doubtless, there will be confusion of thought. Is it in honour or in execration that on the fifth of November the feu d'artifice are sent up? To blow up an English Parliament, was it a sin or a noble deed?"

Japp chuckled.

"Some people would say undoubtedly the latter."

Turning off the main road, the two men passed into the comparative quiet of a mews. They had been dining together and were now taking a short cut to Hercule Poirot's flat.

As they walked along the sound of squibs was still heard periodically. An occasional shower of golden rain illuminated the sky.

"Good night for a murder," remarked Japp with professional interest. "Nobody would hear a shot, for instance, on a night like this."

"It has always seemed odd to me that more criminals do not take advantage of the fact," said Hercule Poirot.

"Do you know, Poirot, I almost wish sometimes that you would commit a murder."

"Mon cher!"

"Yes, I'd like to see just how you'd set about it."

"My dear Japp, if I committed a murder you would not have the least chance of seeing—how I set about it! You would not even be aware, probably, that a murder had been committed."

Japp laughed good-humouredly and affectionately.

"Cocky little devil, aren't you?" he said indulgently.

II

At half past eleven the following morning, Hercule Poirot's telephone rang.

" 'Allo? 'Allo?"

"Hallo, that you, Poirot?"

"Oui, c'est moi."

"Japp speaking here. Remember we came home last night through Bardsley Gardens Mews?"

"Yes?"

"And that we talked about how easy it would be to shoot a person with all those squibs and crackers and the rest of it going off?"

"Certainly."

"Well, there was a suicide in that mews. No. 14. A young widow— Mrs. Allen. I'm going round there now. Like to come?"

"Excuse me, but does someone of your eminence, my dear friend, usually get sent to a case of suicide?"

"Sharp fellow. No—he doesn't. As a matter of fact our doctor seems to think there's something funny about this. Will you come? I kind of feel you ought to be in on it."

"Certainly I will come. No. 14, you say?"

"That's right."

III

Poirot arrived at No. 14 Bardsley Gardens Mews almost at the same moment as a car drew up containing Japp and three other men.

No. 14 was clearly marked out as the centre of interest. A big circle of people, chauffeurs, their wives, errand boys, loafers, well-dressed passersby and innumerable children were drawn up all staring at No. 14 with open mouths and a fascinated stare.

A police constable in uniform stood on the step and did his best to keep back the curious. Alert-looking young men with cameras were busy and surged forward as Japp alighted.

"Nothing for you now," said Japp, brushing them aside. He nodded to Poirot. "So here you are. Let's get inside."

They passed in quickly, the door shut behind them and they found themselves squeezed together at the foot of a ladderlike flight of stairs.

A man came to the top of the staircase, recognized Japp and said:

"Up here, sir."

Japp and Poirot mounted the stairs.

The man at the stairhead opened a door on the left and they found themselves in a small bedroom.

"Thought you'd like me to run over the chief points, sir."

"Quite right, Jameson," said Japp. "What about it?"

Divisional Inspector Jameson took up the tale.

"Deceased's a Mrs. Allen, sir. Lived here with a friend—a Miss Plenderleith. Miss Plenderleith was away staying in the country and returned this morning. She let herself in with her key, was surprised to find no one about. A woman usually comes in at nine o'clock to do for them. She went upstairs first into her own room (that's this room) then across the landing to her friend's room. Door was locked on the inside. She rattled the handle, knocked and called, but couldn't get any answer. In the end getting alarmed she rang up the police station. That was at ten forty-five. We came along at once and forced the door open. Mrs. Allen was lying in a heap on the ground shot through the head. There was an automatic in her hand—a Webley .25—and it looked a clear case of suicide."

"Where is Miss Plenderleith now?"

"She's downstairs in the sitting room, sir. A very cool, efficient young lady, I should say. Got a head on her."

"I'll talk to her presently. I'd better see Brett now."

Accompanied by Poirot he crossed the landing and entered the opposite room. A tall, elderly man looked up and nodded.

"Hallo, Japp, glad you've got here. Funny business, this."

Japp advanced towards him. Hercule Poirot sent a quick searching glance round the room.

It was much larger than the room they had just quitted. It had a built-out bay window, and whereas the other room had been a bedroom pure and simple, this was emphatically a bedroom disguised as a sitting room.

The walls were silver and the ceiling emerald green. There were curtains of a modernistic pattern in silver and green. There was a divan covered with a shimmering emerald green silk quilt and numbers of gold and silver cushions. There was a tall antique walnut bureau, a walnut tallboy, and several modern chairs of gleaming chromium. On a low glass table there was a big ashtray full of cigarette stubs.

Delicately Hercule Poirot sniffed the air. Then he joined Japp where the latter stood looking down at the body.

In a heap on the floor, lying as she had fallen from one of the chromium chairs, was the body of a young woman of perhaps twenty-seven. She had fair hair and delicate features. There was very little makeup on the face. It was a pretty, wistful, perhaps slightly stupid face. On the left side of the head was a mass of congealed blood. The fingers of the right hand were clasped round a small pistol. The woman was dressed in a simple frock of dark green high to the neck.

"Well, Brett, what's the trouble?"

Japp was looking down also at the huddled figure.

"Position's all right," said the doctor. "If she shot herself she'd probably have slipped from the chair into just that position. The door was locked and the window was fastened on the inside."

"That's all right, you say. Then what's wrong?"

"Take a look at the pistol. I haven't handled it—waiting for the fingerprint men. But you can see quite well what I mean."

Together Poirot and Japp knelt down and examined the pistol closely.

"I see what you mean," said Japp rising. "It's in the curve of her hand. It looks as though she's holding it—but as a matter of fact she isn't holding it. Anything else?"

"Plenty. She's got the pistol in her right hand. Now take a look at the wound. The pistol was held close to the head just above the left ear—the left ear, mark you."

"H'm," said Japp. "That does seem to settle it. She couldn't hold a pistol and fire it in that position with her right hand?"

"Plumb impossible, I should say. You might get your arm round but I doubt if you could fire the shot."

"That seems pretty obvious then. Someone else shot her and tried to make it look like suicide. What about the locked door and window, though?"

Inspector Jameson answered this.

"Window was closed and bolted, sir, but although the door was locked we haven't been able to find the key."

Japp nodded.

"Yes, that was a bad break. Whoever did it locked the door when he left and hoped the absence of the key wouldn't be noticed."

Poirot murmured:

"C'est bête, ça!"

"Oh, come now, Poirot, old man, you mustn't judge everybody else by the light of your shining intellect! As a matter of fact that's the sort of little detail that's quite apt to be overlooked. Door's locked. People break in. Woman found dead—pistol in her hand—clear case of suicide—she locked herself in to do it. They don't go hunting about for keys. As a matter of fact, Miss Plenderleith's sending for the police was lucky. She might have got one or two of the chauffeurs to come and burst in the door—and then the key question would have been overlooked altogether."

"Yes, I suppose that is true," said Hercule Poirot. "It would have been many people's natural reaction. The police, they are the last resource, are they not?"

He was still staring down at the body.

"Anything strike you?" Japp asked.

The question was careless but his eyes were keen and attentive.

Hercule Poirot shook his head slowly.

"I was looking at her wristwatch."

He bent over and just touched it with a fingertip. It was a dainty jewelled affair on a black moiré strap on the wrist of the hand that held the pistol.

"Rather a swell piece that," observed Japp. "Must have cost money!" He cocked his head inquiringly at Poirot. "Something in that maybe?"

"It is possible—yes."

Poirot strayed across to the writing bureau. It was the kind that has a front flap that lets down. This was daintily set out to match the general colour scheme.

There was a somewhat massive silver inkstand in the centre, in front of it a handsome green lacquer blotter. To the left of the blotter was an emerald glass pen tray containing a silver penholder—a stick of green sealing wax, a pencil and two stamps. On the right of the blotter was a movable calendar giving the day of the week, date and month. There was also a little glass jar of shot and standing in it a flamboyant green quill pen. Poirot seemed interested in the pen. He took it out and looked at it but the quill was innocent of ink. It was clearly a decoration—nothing more. The silver pen-holder with the ink-stained nib was the one in use. His eyes strayed to the calendar.

"Tuesday, November fifth," said Japp. "Yesterday. That's all correct."

He turned to Brett.

"How long has she been dead?"

"She was killed at eleven thirty-three yesterday evening," said Brett promptly.

Then he grinned as he saw Japp's surprised face.

"Sorry, old boy," he said. "Had to do the super doctor of fiction! As a matter of fact eleven is about as near as I can put it—with a margin of about an hour either way."

"Oh, I thought the wristwatch might have stopped—or something."

"It's stopped all right, but it's stopped at a quarter past four."

"And I suppose she couldn't have been killed possibly at a quarter past four."

"You can put that right out of your mind."

Poirot had turned back the cover of the blotter.

"Good idea," said Japp. "But no luck."

The blotter showed an innocent white sheet of blotting paper. Poirot turned over the leaves but they were all the same.

He turned his attention to the wastepaper basket.

It contained two or three torn-up letters and circulars. They were only torn once and were easily reconstructed. An appeal for money from some society for assisting ex-servicemen, an invitation to a cocktail party on November 3rd, an appointment with a dressmaker. The circulars were an announcement of a furrier's sale and a catalogue from a department store.

"Nothing there," said Japp.

"No, it is odd . . ." said Poirot.

"You mean they usually leave a letter when it's suicide?"

"Exactly."

"In fact, one more proof that it isn't suicide."

He moved away.

"I'll have my men get to work now. We'd better go down and interview this Miss Plenderleith. Coming, Poirot?"

Poirot still seemed fascinated by the writing bureau and its appointments.

He left the room, but at the door his eyes went back once more to the flaunting emerald quill pen.

IV

At the foot of the narrow flight of stairs a door gave admission to a large-sized living room—actually the converted stable. In this room, the walls of which were finished in a roughened plaster effect and on which hung etchings and woodcuts, two people were sitting.

One, in a chair near the fireplace, her hand stretched out to the blaze, was a dark efficient-looking young woman of twenty-seven or -eight. The other, an elderly woman of ample proportions who carried a string bag, was panting and talking when the two men entered the room.

"—and as I said, Miss, such a turn it gave me I nearly dropped down where I stood. And to think that this morning of all mornings—"

The other cut her short.

"That will do, Mrs. Pierce. These gentlemen are police officers, I think."

"Miss Plenderleith?" asked Japp, advancing.

The girl nodded.

"That is my name. This is Mrs. Pierce who comes in to work for us every day."

The irrepressible Mrs. Pierce broke out again.

"And as I was saying to Miss Plenderleith, to think that this morning of all mornings, my sister's Louisa Maud should have been took with a fit and me the only one handy and as I say flesh and blood is flesh and blood, and I didn't think Mrs. Allen would mind, though I never likes to disappoint my ladies—"

Japp broke in with some dexterity.

"Quite so, Mrs. Pierce. Now perhaps you would take Inspector Jameson into the kitchen and give him a brief statement."

Having then got rid of the voluble Mrs. Pierce, who departed with Jameson talking thirteen to the dozen, Japp turned his attention once more to the girl.

"I am Chief Inspector Japp. Now, Miss Plenderleith, I should like to know all you can tell me about this business."

"Certainly. Where shall I begin?"

Her self-possession was admirable. There were no signs of grief or shock save for an almost unnatural rigidity of manner.

"You arrived this morning at what time?"

"I think it was just before half past ten. Mrs. Pierce, the old liar, wasn't here, I found—"

"Is that a frequent occurrence?"

Jane Plenderleith shrugged her shoulders.

"About twice a week she turns up at twelve—or not at all. She's supposed to come at nine. Actually, as I say, twice a week she either 'comes over queer,' or else some member of her family is overtaken by sickness. All these daily women are like that—fail you now and again. She's not bad as they go."

"You've had her long?"

"Just over a month. Our last one pinched things."

"Please go on, Miss Plenderleith."

"I paid off the taxi, carried in my suitcase, looked round for Mrs. P., couldn't see her and went upstairs to my room. I tidied up a bit then I went across to Barbara—Mrs. Allen—and found the door locked. I rattled the handle and knocked but could get no reply. I came downstairs and rang up the police station."

"Pardon!" Poirot interposed a quick, deft question. "It did not occur to you to try and break down the door—with the help of one of the chauffeurs in the mews, say?"

Her eyes turned to him—cool, grey-green eyes. Her glance seemed to sweep over him quickly and appraisingly.

"No, I don't think I thought of that. If anything was wrong, it seemed to me that the police were the people to send for."

"Then you thought—pardon, mademoiselle—that there was something wrong?"

"Naturally."

"Because you could not get a reply to your knocks? But possibly your friend might have taken a sleeping draught or something of that kind—"

"She didn't take sleeping draughts."

The reply came sharply.

"Or she might have gone away and locked her door before going?"

"Why should she lock it? In any case she would have left a note for me."

"And she did not—leave a note for you? You are quite sure of that?"

"Of course I am sure of it. I should have seen it at once."

The sharpness of her tone was accentuated.

Japp said:

"You didn't try and look through the keyhole, Miss Plenderleith?"

"No," said Jane Plenderleith thoughtfully. "I never thought of that. But I couldn't have seen anything, could I? Because the key would have been in it?"

Her inquiring gaze, innocent, wide-eyed, met Japp's. Poirot smiled suddenly to himself.

  The Plymouth Express Affair & Other Stories

"You did quite right, of course, Miss Plenderleith," said Japp. "I suppose you'd no reason to believe that your friend was likely to commit suicide?"

"Oh, no."

"She hadn't seemed worried—or distressed in any way?"

There was a pause—an appreciable pause before the girl answered.

"No."

"Did you know she had a pistol?"

Jane Plenderleith nodded.

"Yes, she had it out in India. She always kept it in a drawer in her room."

"H'm. Got a licence for it?"

"I imagine so. I don't know for certain."

"Now, Miss Plenderleith, will you tell me all you can about Mrs. Allen, how long you've known her, where her relations are—everything in fact."

Jane Plenderleith nodded.

"I've known Barbara about five years. I met her first travelling abroad—in Egypt to be exact. She was on her way home from India. I'd been at the British School in Athens for a bit and was having a few weeks in Egypt before going home. We were on a Nile cruise together. We made friends, decided we liked each other. I was looking at the time for someone to share a flat or a tiny house with me. Barbara was alone in the world. We thought we'd get on well together."

"And you did get on well together?" asked Poirot.

"Very well. We each had our own friends—Barbara was more social in her likings—my friends were more of the artistic kind. It probably worked better that way."

Poirot nodded. Japp went on:

"What do you know about Mrs. Allen's family and her life before she met you?"

Jane Plenderleith shrugged her shoulders.

"Not very much really. Her maiden name was Armitage, I believe."

"Her husband?"

"I don't fancy that he was anything to write home about. He drank, I think. I gather he died a year or two after the marriage. There was one child, a little girl, which died when it was three years old. Barbara didn't talk much about her husband. I believe she married him in India when she was about seventeen. Then they went off to Borneo or one of the godforsaken spots you send ne'er-do-wells to—but as it was obviously a painful subject I didn't refer to it."

"Do you know if Mrs. Allen was in any financial difficulties?"

"No, I'm sure she wasn't."

"Not in debt—anything of that kind?"

"Oh, no! I'm sure she wasn't in that kind of a jam."

"Now there's another question I must ask—and I hope you won't be upset about it, Miss Plenderleith. Had Mrs. Allen any particular man friend or men friends?"

Jane Plenderleith answered coolly:

"Well, she was engaged to be married if that answers your question."

"What is the name of the man she was engaged to?"

"Charles Laverton-West. He's M.P. for some place in Hampshire."

"Had she known him long?"

"A little over a year."

"And she has been engaged to him—how long?"

"Two—no—nearer three months."

"As far as you know there has not been any quarrel?"

Miss Plenderleith shook her head.

"No. I should have been surprised if there had been anything of that sort. Barbara wasn't the quarrelling kind."

"How long is it since you last saw Mrs. Allen?"

"Friday last, just before I went away for the weekend."

"Mrs. Allen was remaining in town?"

"Yes. She was going out with her fiancé on the Sunday, I believe."

"And you yourself, where did you spend the weekend?"

"At Laidells Hall, Laidells, Essex."

"And the name of the people with whom you were staying?"

"Mr. and Mrs. Bentinck."

"You only left them this morning?"

"Yes."

"You must have left very early?"

"Mr. Bentinck motored me up. He starts early because he has to get to the city by ten."

"I see."

Japp nodded comprehendingly. Miss Plenderleith's replies had all been crisp and convincing.

Poirot in his turn put a question.

"What is your own opinion of Mr. Laverton-West?"

The girl shrugged her shoulders.

"Does that matter?"

"No, it does not matter, perhaps, but I should like to have your opinion."

"I don't know that I've thought about him one way or the other. He's young—not more than thirty-one or -two—ambitious—a good public speaker—means to get on in the world."

"That is on the credit side—and on the debit?"

"Well," Miss Plenderleith considered for a moment or two. "In my opinion he's commonplace—his ideas are not particularly original—and he's slightly pompous."

"Those are not very serious faults, mademoiselle," said Poirot, smiling.

"Don't you think so?"

Her tone was slightly ironic.

"They might be to you."

He was watching her, saw her look a little disconcerted. He pursued his advantage.

"But to Mrs. Allen—no, she would not notice them."

"You're perfectly right. Barbara thought he was wonderful—took him entirely at his own valuation."

Poirot said gently:

"You were fond of your friend?"

He saw the hand clench on her knee, the tightening of the line of the jaw, yet the answer came in a matter-of-fact voice free from emotion.

"You are quite right. I was."

Japp said:

"Just one other thing, Miss Plenderleith. You and she didn't have a quarrel? There was no upset between you?"

"None whatever."

"Not over this engagement business?"

"Certainly not. I was glad she was able to be so happy about it."

There was a momentary pause, then Japp said:

"As far as you know, did Mrs. Allen have any enemies?"

This time there was a definite interval before Jane Plenderleith replied. When she did so, her tone had altered very slightly.

"I don't know quite what you mean by enemies?"

"Anyone, for instance, who would profit by her death?"

"Oh, no, that would be ridiculous. She had a very small income anyway."

"And who inherits that income?"

Jame Plenderleith's voice sounded mildly surprised as she said:

"Do you know, I really don't know. I shouldn't be surprised if I did. That is, if she ever made a will."

"And no enemies in any other sense?" Japp slid off to another aspect quickly. "People with a grudge against her?"

"I don't think anyone had a grudge against her. She was a very gentle creature, always anxious to please. She had a really sweet, lovable nature."

For the first time that hard, matter-of-fact voice broke a little. Poirot nodded gently.

Japp said:

"So it amounts to this—Mrs. Allen has been in good spirits lately, she wasn't in any financial difficulty, she was engaged to be married and was happy in her engagement. There was nothing in the world to make her commit suicide. That's right, isn't it?"

There was a momentary silence before Jane said:

"Yes."

Japp rose.

"Excuse me, I must have a word with Inspector Jameson."

He left the room.

Hercule Poirot remained tête à tête with Jane Plenderleith.

V

For a few minutes there was silence.

Jane Plenderleith shot a swift appraising glance at the little man, but after that she stared in front of her and did not speak. Yet a consciousness of his presence showed itself in a certain nervous tension. Her body was still but not relaxed. When at last Poirot did break the silence the mere sound of his voice seemed to give her a certain relief. In an agreeable everyday voice he asked a question.

"When did you light the fire, mademoiselle?"

"The fire?" Her voice sounded vague and rather absentminded. "Oh, as soon as I arrived this morning."

"Before you went upstairs or afterwards?"

"Before."

"I see. Yes, naturally . . . And it was already laid—or did you have to lay it?"

"It was laid. I only had to put a match to it."

There was a slight impatience in her voice. Clearly she suspected him of making conversation. Possibly that was what he was doing. At any rate he went on in quiet conversational tones.

"But your friend—in her room I noticed there was a gas fire only?"

Jane Plenderleith answered mechanically.

"This is the only coal fire we have—the others are all gas fires."

"And you cook with gas, too?"

"I think everyone does nowadays."

"True. It is much labour saving."

The little interchange died down. Jane Plenderleith tapped on the ground with her shoe. Then she said abruptly:

"That man—Chief Inspector Japp—is he considered clever?"

"He is very sound. Yes, he is well thought of. He works hard and painstakingly and very little escapes him."

"I wonder—" muttered the girl.

Poirot watched her. His eyes looked very green in the firelight. He asked quietly:

"It was a great shock to you, your friend's death?"

"Terrible."

She spoke with abrupt sincerity.

"You did not expect it—no?"

"Of course not."

"So that it seemed to you at first, perhaps, that it was impossible—that it could not be?"

The quiet sympathy of his tone seemed to break down Jane Plenderleith's defences. She replied eagerly, naturally, without stiffness.

"That's just it. Even if Barbara did kill herself, I can't imagine her killing herself that way."

"Yet she had a pistol?"

Jane Plenderleith made an impatient gesture.

"Yes, but that pistol was a—oh! a hang over. She'd been in out-of-the-way places. She kept it out of habit—not with any other idea. I'm sure of that."

"Ah! and why are you sure of that?"

"Oh, because of the things she said."

"Such as—?"

His voice was very gentle and friendly. It led her on subtly.

"Well, for instance, we were discussing suicide once and she said much the easiest way would be to turn the gas on and stuff up all the cracks and just go to bed. I said I thought that would be impossible—to lie there waiting. I said I'd far rather shoot myself. And she said no, she could never shoot herself. She'd be too frightened in case it didn't come off and anyway she said she'd hate the bang."

"I see," said Poirot. "As you say, it is odd . . . Because, as you have just told me, there was a gas fire in her room."

Jane Plenderleith looked at him, slightly startled.

"Yes, there was . . . I can't understand—no, I can't understand why she didn't do it that way."

Poirot shook his head.

"Yes, it seems—odd—not natural somehow."

"The whole thing doesn't seem natural. I still can't believe she killed herself. I suppose it must be suicide?"

"Well, there is one other possibility."

"What do you mean?"

Poirot looked straight at her.

"It might be—murder."

"Oh, no?" Jane Plenderleith shrank back. "Oh no! What a horrible suggestion."

"Horrible, perhaps, but does it strike you as an impossible one?"

"But the door was locked on the inside. So was the window."

"The door was locked—yes. But there is nothing to show if it were locked from the inside or the outside. You see, the key was missing."

"But then—if it is missing . . ." She took a minute or two. "Then it must have been locked from the outside. Otherwise it would be somewhere in the room."

"Ah, but it may be. The room has not been thoroughly searched yet, remember. Or it may have been thrown out of the window and somebody may have picked it up."

"Murder!" said Jane Plenderleith. She turned over the possibility, her dark clever face eager on the scent. "I believe you're right."

"But if it were murder there would have been a motive. Do you know of a motive, mademoiselle?"

Slowly she shook her head. And yet, in spite of the denial, Poirot again got the impression that Jane Plenderleith was deliberately keeping something back. The door opened and Japp came in.

Poirot rose.

"I have been suggesting to Miss Plenderleith," he said, "that her friend's death was not suicide."

Japp looked momentarily put out. He cast a glance of reproach at Poirot.

"It's a bit early to say anything definite," he remarked. "We've always got to take all possibilities into account, you understand. That's all there is to it at the moment."

Jane Plenderleith replied quietly.

"I see."

Japp came towards her.

"Now then, Miss Plenderleith, have you ever seen this before?"

On the palm of his hand he held out a small oval of dark blue enamel.

Jane Plenderleith shook her head.

"No, never."

"It's not yours nor Mrs. Allen's?"

"No. It's not the kind of thing usually worn by our sex, is it?"

"Oh! so you recognize it."

"Well, it's pretty obvious, isn't it? That's half of a man's cuff link."

<h2 style="text-align:center">VI</h2>

"That young woman's too cocky by half," Japp complained.

The two men were once more in Mrs. Allen's bedroom. The body had been photographed and removed and the fingerprint man had done his work and departed.

"It would be unadvisable to treat her as a fool," agreed Poirot. "She most emphatically is not a fool. She is, in fact, a particularly clever and competent young woman."

"Think she did it?" asked Japp with a momentary ray of hope. "She might have, you know. We'll have to get her alibi looked into. Some quarrel over this young man—this budding M.P. She's rather too scathing about him, I think! Sounds fishy. Rather as though she were sweet on him herself and he'd turned her down. She's the kind that would bump anyone off if she felt like it, and keep her head while she was doing it, too. Yes, we'll have to look into that alibi. She had it very pat and after all Essex isn't very far away. Plenty of trains. Or a fast car. It's worthwhile finding out if she went to bed with a headache for instance last night."

"You are right," agreed Poirot.

"In any case," continued Japp, "she's holding out on us. Eh? Didn't you feel that too? That young woman knows something."

Poirot nodded thoughtfully.

"Yes, that could be clearly seen."

"That's always a difficulty in these cases," Japp complained. "People will hold their tongues—sometimes out of the most honourable motives."

"For which one can hardly blame them, my friend."

"No, but it makes it much harder for us," Japp grumbled.

"It merely displays to its full advantage your ingenuity," Poirot consoled him. "What about fingerprints, by the way?"

"Well, it's murder all right. No prints whatever on the pistol. Wiped clean before being placed in her hand. Even if she managed to wind her arm round her head in some marvellous acrobatic fashion she could hardly fire off a pistol without hanging on to it and she couldn't wipe it after she was dead."

"No, no, an outside agency is clearly indicated."

"Otherwise the prints are disappointing. None on the door handle. None on the window. Suggestive, eh? Plenty of Mrs. Allen's all over the place."

"Did Jameson get anything?"

"Out of the daily woman? No. She talked a lot but she didn't really know much. Confirmed the fact that Allen and Plenderleith were on good terms. I've sent Jameson out to make inquiries in the

 The Plymouth Express Affair & Other Stories

mews. We'll have to have a word with Mr. Laverton-West too. Find out where he was and what he was doing last night. In the meantime we'll have a look through her papers."

He set to without more ado. Occasionally he grunted and tossed something over to Poirot. The search did not take long. There were not many papers in the desk and what there were were neatly arranged and docketed.

Finally Japp leant back and uttered a sigh.

"Not very much, is there?"

"As you say."

"Most of it quite straightforward—receipted bills, a few bills as yet unpaid—nothing particularly outstanding. Social stuff—invitations. Notes from friends. These—" he laid his hand on a pile of seven or eight letters—"and her cheque book and passbook. Anything strike you there?"

"Yes, she was overdrawn."

"Anything else?"

Poirot smiled.

"Is it an examination that you put me through? But yes, I noticed what you are thinking of. Two hundred pounds drawn to self three months ago—and two hundred pounds drawn out yesterday—"

"And nothing on the counterfoil of the cheque book. No other cheques to self except small sums—fifteen pounds the highest. And I'll tell you this—there's no such sum of money in the house. Four pounds ten in a handbag and an odd shilling or two in another bag. That's pretty clear, I think."

"Meaning that she paid that sum away yesterday."

"Yes. Now who did she pay it to?"

The door opened and Inspector Jameson entered.

"Well, Jameson, get anything?"

"Yes, sir, several things. To begin with, nobody actually heard the shot. Two or three women say they did because they want to think they did—but that's all there is to it. With all those fireworks going off there isn't a dog's chance."

Japp grunted.

"Don't suppose there is. Go on."

"Mrs. Allen was at home most of yesterday afternoon and evening. Came in about five o'clock. Then she went out again about six but only to the postbox at the end of the mews. At about nine thirty a car drove up—Standard Swallow saloon—and a man got out. Description about forty-five, well set up military-looking gent, dark blue overcoat, bowler hat, toothbrush moustache. James Hogg, chauffeur from No. 18 says he's seen him calling on Mrs. Allen before."

"Forty-five," said Japp. "Can't very well be Laverton-West."

"This man, whoever he was, stayed here for just under an hour. Left at about ten twenty. Stopped in the doorway to speak to Mrs. Allen. Small boy, Frederick Hogg, was hanging about quite near and heard what he said."

"And what did he say?"

" 'Well, think it over and let me know.' And then she said something and he answered: 'All right. So long.' After that he got in his car and drove away."

"That was at ten twenty," said Poirot thoughtfully.

Japp rubbed his nose.

"Then at ten twenty Mrs. Allen was still alive," he said. "What next?"

"Nothing more, sir, as far as I can learn. The chauffeur at No. 22 got in at half-past ten and he'd promised his kids to let off some fireworks for them. They'd been waiting for him—and all the other kids in the mews too. He let 'em off and everybody around about was busy watching them. After that everyone went to bed."

"And nobody else was seen to enter No. 14?"

"No—but that's not to say they didn't. Nobody would have noticed."

"H'm," said Japp. "That's true. Well, we'll have to get hold of this 'military gentleman with the toothbrush moustache.' It's pretty clear that he was the last person to see her alive. I wonder who he was?"

"Miss Plenderleith might tell us," suggested Poirot.

"She might," said Japp gloomily. "On the other hand she might not. I've no doubt she could tell us a good deal if she liked. What about you, Poirot, old boy? You were alone with her for a bit. Didn't you trot out that Father Confessor manner of yours that sometimes makes such a hit?"

Poirot spread out his hands.

"Alas, we talked only of gas fires."

"Gas fires—gas fires." Japp sounded disgusted. "What's the matter with you, old cock? Ever since you've been here the only things you've taken an interest in are quill pens and wastepaper baskets. Oh, yes, I saw you having a quiet look into the one downstairs. Anything in it?"

Poirot sighed.

"A catalogue of bulbs and an old magazine."

"What's the idea, anyway? If anyone wants to throw away an incriminating document or whatever it is you have in mind they're not likely just to pitch it into a wastepaper basket."

"That is very true what you say there. Only something quite unimportant would be thrown away like that."

Poirot spoke meekly. Nevertheless Japp looked at him suspiciously.

"Well," he said. "I know what I'm going to do next. What about you?"

"Eh bien," said Poirot. "I shall complete my search for the unimportant. There is still the dustbin."

He skipped nimbly out of the room. Japp looked after him with an air of disgust.

"Potty," he said. "Absolutely potty."

Inspector Jameson preserved a respectful silence. His face said with British superiority: "Foreigners!"

Aloud he said:

"So that's Mr. Hercule Poirot! I've heard of him."

"Old friend of mine," explained Japp. "Not half as balmy as he looks, mind you. All the same he's getting on now."

"Gone a bit gaga as they say, sir," suggested Inspector Jameson. "Ah well, age will tell."

"All the same," said Japp, "I wish I knew what he was up to."

He walked over to the writing table and stared uneasily at an emerald green quill pen.

VII

Japp was just engaging his third chauffeur's wife in conversation when Poirot, walking noiselessly as a cat, suddenly appeared at his elbow.

"Whew, you made me jump," said Japp. "Got anything?"

"Not what I was looking for."

Japp turned back to Mrs. James Hogg.

"And you say you've seen this gentleman before?"

"Oh, yes sir. And my husband too. We knew him at once."

"Now look here, Mrs. Hogg, you're a shrewd woman, I can see. I've no doubt that you know all about everyone in the mews. And you're a woman of judgment—unusually good judgment, I can tell that—" Unblushingly he repeated this remark for the third time. Mrs. Hogg bridled slightly and assumed an expression of superhuman intelligence. "Give me a line on those two young women—Mrs. Allen and Miss Plenderleith. What were they like? Gay? Lots of parties? That sort of thing?"

"Oh, no sir, nothing of the kind. They went out a good bit—Mrs. Allen especially—but they're class, if you know what I mean. Not like some as I could name down the other end. I'm sure the way that Mrs. Stevens goes on—if she is a Mrs. at all which I doubt—well I shouldn't like to tell you what goes on there—I. . . ."

"Quite so," said Japp, dexterously stopping the flow. "Now that's very important what you've told me. Mrs. Allen and Miss Plenderleith were well liked, then?"

"Oh yes, sir, very nice ladies, both of them—especially Mrs. Allen. Always spoke a nice word to the children, she did. Lost her own little girl, I believe, poor dear. Ah well, I've buried three myself. And what I say is . . ."

"Yes, yes, very sad. And Miss Plenderleith?"

"Well, of course she was a nice lady too, but much more abrupt if you know what I mean. Just go by with a nod, she would, and not stop to pass the time of day. But I've nothing against her—nothing at all."

"She and Mrs. Allen got on well together?"

"Oh, yes sir. No quarrelling—nothing like that. Very happy and contented they were—I'm sure Mrs. Pierce will bear me out."

"Yes, we've talked to her. Do you know Mrs. Allen's fiancé by sight?"

"The gentleman she's going to marry? Oh, yes. He's been here quite a bit off and on. Member of Parliament, they do say."

"It wasn't he who came last night?"

"No, sir, it was not." Mrs. Hogg drew herself up. A note of excitement disguised beneath intense primness came into her voice. "And if you ask me, sir, what you are thinking is all wrong. Mrs. Allen wasn't that kind of lady, I'm sure. It's true there was no one in the house, but I do not believe anything of the kind—I said so to Hogg only this morning. 'No, Hogg,' I said, 'Mrs. Allen was a lady—a real lady—so don't go suggesting things'—knowing what a man's mind is, if you'll excuse my mentioning it. Always coarse in their ideas."

Passing this insult by, Japp proceeded:

"You saw him arrive and you saw him leave—that's so, isn't it?"

"That's so, sir."

"And you didn't hear anything else? Any sounds of a quarrel?"

"No, sir, nor likely to. Not, that is to say, that such things couldn't be heard—because the contrary to that is well-known—and down the other end the way Mrs. Stevens goes for that poor frightened maid of hers is common talk—and one and all we've advised her not to stand it, but there, the wages is good—temper of the devil she may have but pays for it—thirty shillings a week. . . ."

Japp said quickly:

"But you didn't hear anything of the kind at No. 14?"

"No, sir. Nor likely to with fireworks popping off here, there and everywhere and my Eddie with his eyebrows singed off as near as nothing."

"This man left at ten twenty—that's right, is it?"

"It might be, sir. I couldn't say myself. But Hogg says so and he's a very reliable, steady man."

"You actually saw him leave. Did you hear what he said?"

"No, sir. I wasn't near enough for that. Just saw him from my windows, standing in the doorway talking to Mrs. Allen."

"See her too?"

"Yes, sir, she was standing just inside the doorway."

"Notice what she was wearing?"

"Now really, sir, I couldn't say. Not noticing particularly as it were."

Poirot said:

"You did not even notice if she was wearing day dress or evening dress?"

"No, sir, I can't say I did."

Poirot looked thoughtfully up at the window above and then across to No. 14. He smiled and for a moment his eye caught Japp's.

          The Plymouth Express Affair & Other Stories

"And the gentleman?"

"He was in a dark-blue overcoat and a bowler hat. Very smart and well set up."

Japp asked a few more questions and then proceeded to his next interview. This was with Master Frederick Hogg, an impish-faced, bright-eyed lad, considerably swollen with self-importance.

"Yes, sir. I heard them talking. 'Think it over and let me know,' the gent said. Pleasant like, you know. And then she said something and he answered, 'All right. So long.' And he got into the car—I was holding the door open but he didn't give me nothing," said Master Hogg with a slight tinge of depression in his tone. "And he drove away."

"You didn't hear what Mrs. Allen said?"

"No, sir, can't say I did."

"Can you tell me what she was wearing? What colour, for instance?"

"Couldn't say, sir. You see, I didn't really see her. She must have been round behind the door."

"Just so," said Japp. "Now look here, my boy, I want you to think and answer my next question very carefully. If you don't know and can't remember, say so. Is that clear?"

"Yes, sir."

Master Hogg looked at him eagerly.

"Which of 'em closed the door, Mrs. Allen or the gentleman?"

"The front door?"

"The front door, naturally."

The child reflected. His eyes screwed themselves up in an effort of remembrance.

"Think the lady probably did—No, she didn't. He did. Pulled it to with a bit of a bang and jumped into the car quick. Looked as though he had a date somewhere."

"Right. Well, young man, you seem a bright kind of shaver. Here's sixpence for you."

Dismissing Master Hogg, Japp turned to his friend. Slowly with one accord they nodded.

"Could be!" said Japp.

"There are possibilities," agreed Poirot.

His eyes shone with a green light. They looked like a cat's.

VIII

On reentering the sitting room of No. 14, Japp wasted no time in beating about the bush. He came straight to the point.

"Now look here, Miss Plenderleith, don't you think it's better to spill the beans here and now. It's going to come to that in the end."

Jane Plenderleith raised her eyebrows. She was standing by the mantelpiece, gently warming one foot at the fire.

"I really don't know what you mean."

"Is that quite true, Miss Plenderleith?"

She shrugged her shoulders.

"I've answered all your questions. I don't see what more I can do."

"Well, it's my opinion you could do a lot more—if you chose."

"That's only an opinion, though, isn't it, Chief Inspector?"

Japp grew rather red in the face.

"I think," said Poirot, "that mademoiselle would appreciate better the reason for your questions if you told her just how the case stands."

"That's very simple. Now then, Miss Plenderleith, the facts are as follows. Your friend was found shot through the head with a pistol in her hand and the door and the window fastened. That looked like a plain case of suicide. But it wasn't suicide. The medical evidence alone proves that."

"How?"

All her ironic coolness had disappeared. She leaned forward—intent—watching his face.

"The pistol was in her hand—but the fingers weren't grasping it. Moreover there were no fingerprints at all on the pistol. And the angle of the wound makes it impossible that the wound should have been self-inflicted. Then again, she left no letter—rather an unusual thing for a suicide. And though the door was locked the key has not been found."

Jane Plenderleith turned slowly and sat down in a chair facing them.

"So that's it!" she said. "All along I've felt it was impossible that she should have killed herself! I was right! She didn't kill herself. Someone else killed her."

For a moment or two she remained lost in thought. Then she raised her head brusquely.

"Ask me any questions you like," she said. "I will answer them to the best of my ability."

Japp began:

"Last night Mrs. Allen had a visitor. He is described as a man of forty-five, military bearing, toothbrush moustache, smartly dressed and driving a Standard Swallow saloon car. Do you know who that is?"

"I can't be sure, of course, but it sounds like Major Eustace."

"Who is Major Eustace? Tell me all you can about him?"

"He was a man Barbara had known abroad—in India. He turned up about a year ago, and we've seen him on and off since."

"He was a friend of Mrs. Allen's?"

"He behaved like one," said Jane dryly.

"What was her attitude to him?"

"I don't think she really liked him—in fact, I'm sure she didn't."

"But she treated him with outward friendliness?"

"Yes."

"Did she ever seem—think carefully, Miss Plenderleith—afraid of him?"

Jane Plenderleith considered this thoughtfully for a minute or two. Then she said:

"Yes—I think she was. She was always nervous when he was about."

"Did he and Mr. Laverton-West meet at all?"

"Only once, I think. They didn't take to each other much. That is to say, Major Eustace made himself as agreeable as he could to Charles, but Charles wasn't having any. Charles has got a very good nose for anybody who isn't well—quite—quite."

"And Major Eustace was not—what you call—quite—quite?" asked Poirot.

The girl said dryly:

"No, he wasn't. Bit hairy at the heel. Definitely not out of the top drawer."

"Alas—I do not know those two expressions. You mean to say he was not the pukka sahib?"

A fleeting smile passed across Jane Plenderleith's face, but she replied gravely, "No."

"Would it come as a great surprise to you, Miss Plenderleith, if I suggested that this man was blackmailing Mrs. Allen?"

Japp sat forward to observe the result of his suggestion.

He was well satisfied. The girl started forward, the colour rose in her cheeks, she brought down her hand sharply on the arm of her chair.

"So that was it! What a fool I was not to have guessed. Of course!"

"You think the suggestion feasible, mademoiselle?" asked Poirot.

"I was a fool not to have thought of it! Barbara's borrowed small sums off me several times during the last six months. And I've seen her sitting poring over her passbook. I knew she was living well within her income, so I didn't bother, but, of course, if she was paying out sums of money—"

"And it would accord with her general demeanour—yes?" asked Poirot.

"Absolutely. She was nervous. Quite jumpy sometimes. Altogether different from what she used to be."

Poirot said gently:

"Excuse me, but that is not just what you told us before."

"That was different," Jane Plenderleith waved an impatient hand. "She wasn't depressed. I mean she wasn't feeling suicidal or anything like that. But blackmail—yes. I wish she'd told me. I'd have sent him to the devil."

"But he might have gone—not to the devil, but to Mr. Charles Laverton-West?" observed Poirot.

"Yes," said Jane Plenderleith slowly. "Yes . . . that's true. . . ."

"You've no idea of what this man's hold over her may have been?" asked Japp.

The girl shook her head.

"I haven't the faintest idea. I can't believe, knowing Barbara, that it could have been anything really serious. On the other hand—" she paused, then went on. "What I mean is, Barbara was a bit of a simpleton in some ways. She'd be very easily frightened. In fact, she was the kind of girl who would be a positive gift to a blackmailer! The nasty brute!"

She snapped out the last three words with real venom.

"Unfortunately," said Poirot, "the crime seems to have taken place the wrong way round. It is the victim who should kill the blackmailer, not the blackmailer his victim."

Jane Plenderleith frowned a little.

"No—that is true—but I can imagine circumstances—"

"Such as?"

"Supposing Barbara got desperate. She may have threatened him with that silly little pistol of hers. He tries to wrench it away from her and in the struggle he fires it and kills her. Then he's horrified at what he's done and tries to pretend it was suicide."

"Might be," said Japp. "But there's a difficulty."

She looked at him inquiringly.

"Major Eustace (if it was him) left here last night at ten twenty and said goodbye to Mrs. Allen on the doorstep."

"Oh," the girl's face fell. "I see." She paused a minute or two. "But he might have come back later," she said slowly.

"Yes, that is possible," said Poirot.

Japp continued:

"Tell me, Miss Plenderleith, where was Mrs. Allen in the habit of receiving guests, here or in the room upstairs?"

"Both. But this room was used for more communal parties or for my own special friends. You see, the arrangement was that Barbara had the big bedroom and used it as a sitting room as well, and I had the little bedroom and used this room."

"If Major Eustace came by appointment last night, in which room do you think Mrs. Allen would have received him?"

"I think she would probably bring him in here." The girl sounded a little doubtful. "It would be less intimate. On the other hand, if she wanted to write a cheque or anything of that kind, she would probably take him upstairs. There are no writing materials down here."

Japp shook his head.

"There was no question of a cheque. Mrs. Allen drew out two hundred pounds in cash yesterday. And so far we've not been able to find any trace of it in the house."

"And she gave it to that brute? Oh, poor Barbara! Poor, poor Barbara!"

Poirot coughed.

"Unless, as you suggest, it was more or less an accident, it still seems a remarkable fact that he should kill an apparently regular source of income."

"Accident? It wasn't an accident. He lost his temper and saw red and shot her."

"That is how you think it happened?"

"Yes." She added vehemently, "It was murder—murder!"

Poirot said gravely:

"I will not say that you are wrong, mademoiselle."

Japp said:

"What cigarettes did Mrs. Allen smoke?"

"Gaspers. There are some in that box."

Japp opened the box, took out a cigarette and nodded. He slipped the cigarette into his pocket.

"And you, mademoiselle?" asked Poirot.

"The same."

"You do not smoke Turkish?"

"Never."

"Nor Mrs. Allen?"

"No. She didn't like them."

Poirot asked:

"And Mr. Laverton-West. What did he smoke?"

She stared hard at him.

"Charles? What does it matter what he smoked? You're not going to pretend that he killed her?"

Poirot shrugged his shoulders.

"A man has killed the woman he loved before now, mademoiselle."

Jane shook her head impatiently.

"Charles wouldn't kill anybody. He's a very careful man."

"All the same, mademoiselle, it is the careful men who commit the cleverest murders."

She stared at him.

"But not for the motive you have just advanced, M. Poirot."

He bowed his head.

"No, that is true."

Japp rose.

"Well, I don't think that there's much more I can do here. I'd like to have one more look round."

"In case that money should be tucked away somewhere? Certainly. Look anywhere you like. And in my room too—although it isn't likely Barbara would hide it there."

Japp's search was quick but efficient. The living room had given up all its secrets in a very few minutes. Then he went upstairs. Jane Plenderleith sat on the arm of a chair, smoking a cigarette and frowning at the fire. Poirot watched her.

After some minutes, he said quietly:

"Do you know if Mr. Laverton-West is in London at present?"

"I don't know at all. I rather fancy he's in Hampshire with his people. I suppose I ought to have wired him. How dreadful. I forgot."

"It is not easy to remember everything, mademoiselle, when a catastrophe occurs. And after all, the bad news, it will keep. One hears it only too soon."

"Yes, that's true," the girl said absently.

Japp's footsteps were heard descending the stairs. Jane went out to meet him.

"Well?"

Japp shook his head.

"Nothing helpful, I'm afraid, Miss Plenderleith. I've been over the whole house now. Oh, I suppose I'd better just have a look in this cupboard under the stairs."

He caught hold of the handle as he spoke, and pulled.

Jane Plenderleith said:

"It's locked."

Something in her voice made both men look at her sharply.

"Yes," said Japp pleasantly. "I can see it's locked. Perhaps you'll get the key."

The girl was standing as though carved in stone.

"I—I'm not sure where it is."

Japp shot a quick glance at her. His voice continued resolutely pleasant and offhand.

"Dear me, that's too bad. Don't want to splinter the wood, opening it by force. I'll send Jameson out to get an assortment of keys."

She moved forward stiffly.

"Oh," she said. "One minute. It might be—"

She went back into the living room and reappeared a moment later holding a fair-sized key in her hand.

"We keep it locked," she explained, "because one's umbrellas and things have a habit of getting pinched."

"Very wise precaution," said Japp, cheerfully accepting the key.

He turned it in the lock and threw the door open. It was dark inside the cupboard. Japp took out his pocket flashlight and let it play round the inside.

Poirot felt the girl at his side stiffen and stop breathing for a second. His eyes followed the sweep of Japp's torch.

There was not very much in the cupboard. Three umbrellas—one broken, four walking sticks, a set of golf clubs, two tennis racquets, a neatly-folded rug and several sofa cushions in various stages of dilapidation. On the top of these last reposed a small, smart-looking attaché case.

As Japp stretched out a hand towards it, Jane Plenderleith said quickly:

"That's mine. I—it came back with me this morning. So there can't be anything there."

"Just as well to make quite sure," said Japp, his cheery friendliness increasing slightly.

The case was unlocked. Inside it was fitted with shagreen brushes and toilet bottles. There were two magazines in it but nothing else.

Japp examined the whole outfit with meticulous attention. When at last he shut the lid and began a cursory examination of the cushions, the girl gave an audible sigh of relief.

There was nothing else in the cupboard beyond what was plainly to be seen. Japp's examination was soon finished.

He relocked the door and handed the key to Jane Plenderleith.

"Well," he said, "that concludes matters. Can you give me Mr. Laverton-West's address?"

"Farlescombe Hall, Little Ledbury, Hampshire."

"Thank you, Miss Plenderleith. That's all for the present. I may be round again later. By the way, mum's the word. Leave it at suicide as far as the general public's concerned."

"Of course, I quite understand."

She shook hands with them both.

As they walked away down the mews, Japp exploded:

"What the—the hell was there in that cupboard? There was something."

"Yes, there was something."

"And I'll bet ten to one it was something to do with the attaché case! But like the double-dyed mutt I must be, I couldn't find anything. Looked in all the bottles—felt the lining—what the devil could it be?"

Poirot shook his head thoughtfully.

"That girl's in it somehow," Japp went on. "Brought that case back this morning? Not on your life, she didn't! Notice that there were two magazines in it?"

"Yes."

"Well, one of them was for last July!"

IX

It was the following day when Japp walked into Poirot's flat, flung his hat on the table in deep disgust and dropped into a chair.

"Well," he growled. "She's out of it!"

"Who is out of it?"

"Plenderleith. Was playing bridge up to midnight. Host, hostess, naval commander guest and two servants can all swear to that. No doubt about it, we've got to give up any idea of her being concerned in the business. All the same, I'd like to know why she went all hot and bothered about that little attaché case under the stairs. That's something in your line, Poirot. You like solving the kind of triviality that leads nowhere. The Mystery of the Small Attaché Case. Sounds quite promising!"

"I will give you yet another suggestion for a title. The Mystery of the Smell of Cigarette Smoke."

"A bit clumsy for a title. Smell—eh? Was that why you were sniffing so when we first examined the body? I saw you—and heard you! Sniff—sniff—sniff. Thought you had a cold in your head."

"You were entirely in error."

Japp sighed.

"I always thought it was the little grey cells of the brain. Don't tell me the cells of your nose are equally superior to anyone else's."

"No, no, calm yourself."

"I didn't smell any cigarette smoke," went on Japp suspiciously.

"No more did I, my friend."

Japp looked at him doubtfully. Then he extracted a cigarette from his pocket.

"That's the kind Mrs. Allen smoked—gaspers. Six of those stubs were hers. The other three were Turkish."

"Exactly."

"Your wonderful nose knew that without looking at them, I suppose!"

"I assure you my nose does not enter into the matter. My nose registered nothing."

"But the brain cells registered a lot?"

"Well—there were certain indications—do you not think so?"

Japp looked at him sideways.

"Such as?"

"Eh bien, there was very definitely something missing from the room. Also something added, I think . . . And then, on the writing bureau . . ."

"I knew it! We're coming to that damned quill pen!"

"Du tout. The quill pen plays a purely negative rôle."

Japp retreated to safer ground.

"I've got Charles Laverton-West coming to see me at Scotland Yard in half an hour. I thought you might like to be there."

"I should very much."

"And you'll be glad to hear we've tracked down Major Eustace. Got a service flat in the Cromwell Road."

"Excellent."

"And we've got a little to go on there. Not at all a nice person, Major Eustace. After I've seen Laverton-West, we'll go and see him. That suit you?"

"Perfectly."

"Well, come along then."

X

At half past eleven, Charles Laverton-West was ushered into Chief Inspector Japp's room. Japp rose and shook hands.

The M.P. was a man of medium height with a very definite personality. He was clean-shaven, with the mobile mouth of an actor, and the slightly prominent eyes that so often go with the gift of oratory. He was good-looking in a quiet, well-bred way.

Though looking pale and somewhat distressed, his manner was perfectly formal and composed.

He took a seat, laid his gloves and hat on the table and looked towards Japp.

"I'd like to say, first of all, Mr. Laverton-West, that I fully appreciate how distressing this must be to you."

Laverton-West waved this aside.

"Do not let us discuss my feelings. Tell me, Chief Inspector, have you any idea what caused my—Mrs. Allen to take her own life?"

"You yourself cannot help us in any way?"

"No, indeed."

"There was no quarrel? No estrangement of any kind between you?"

"Nothing of the kind. It has been the greatest shock to me."

"Perhaps it will be more understandable, sir, if I tell you that it was not suicide—but murder!"

"Murder?" Charles Laverton-West's eyes popped nearly out of his head. "You say murder?"

"Quite correct. Now, Mr. Laverton-West, have you any idea who might be likely to make away with Mrs. Allen?"

Laverton-West fairly spluttered out his answer.

"No—no, indeed—nothing of the sort! The mere idea is—is unimaginable!"

"She never mentioned any enemies? Anyone who might have a grudge against her?"

"Never."

"Did you know that she had a pistol?"

"I was not aware of the fact."

He looked a little startled.

"Miss Plenderleith says that Mrs. Allen brought this pistol back from abroad with her some years ago."

"Really?"

"Of course, we have only Miss Plenderleith's word for that. It is quite possible that Mrs. Allen felt herself to be in danger from some source and kept the pistol handy for reasons of her own."

Charles Laverton-West shook his head doubtfully. He seemed quite bewildered and dazed.

"What is your opinion of Miss Plenderleith, Mr. Laverton-West? I mean, does she strike you as a reliable, truthful person?"

The other pondered a minute.

"I think so—yes, I should say so."

"You don't like her?" suggested Japp, who had been watching him closely.

"I wouldn't say that. She is not the type of young woman I admire. That sarcastic, independent type is not attractive to me, but I should say she was quite truthful."

"H'm," said Japp. "Do you know a Major Eustace?"

"Eustace? Eustace? Ah, yes, I remember the name. I met him once at Barbara's—Mrs. Allen's. Rather a doubtful customer in my opinion. I said as much to my—to Mrs. Allen. He wasn't the type of man I should have encouraged to come to the house after we were married."

"And what did Mrs. Allen say?"

"Oh! she quite agreed. She trusted my judgment implicitly. A man knows other men better than a woman can do. She explained that she couldn't very well be rude to a man whom she had not seen for some time—I think she felt especially a horror of being snobbish! Naturally, as my wife, she would find a good many of her old associates well—unsuitable, shall we say?"

"Meaning that in marrying you she was bettering her position?" Japp asked bluntly.

Laverton-West held up a well-manicured hand.

"No, no, not quite that. As a matter of fact, Mrs. Allen's mother was a distant relation of my own family. She was fully my equal in birth. But of course, in my position, I have to be especially careful in choosing my friends—and my wife in choosing hers. One is to a certain extent in the limelight."

"Oh, quite," said Japp dryly. He went on, "So you can't help us in any way?"

"No indeed. I am utterly at sea. Barbara! Murdered! It seems incredible."

"Now, Mr. Laverton-West, can you tell me what your own movements were on the night of November fifth?"

"My movements? My movements?"

Laverton-West's voice rose in shrill protest.

"Purely a matter of routine," explained Japp. "We—er—have to ask everybody."

Charles Laverton-West looked at him with dignity.

"I should hope that a man in my position might be exempt."

Japp merely waited.

"I was—now let me see . . . Ah, yes. I was at the House. Left at half past ten. Went for a walk along the Embankment. Watched some of the fireworks."

"Nice to think there aren't any plots of that kind nowadays," said Japp cheerily.

Laverton-West gave him a fish-like stare.

"Then I—er—walked home."

"Reaching home—your London address is Onslow Square, I think—at what time?"

"I hardly know exactly."

"Eleven? Half past?"

"Somewhere about then."

"Perhaps someone let you in."

"No, I have my key."

"Meet anybody whilst you were walking?"

"No—er—really, Chief Inspector, I resent these questions very much!"

"I assure you, it's just a matter of routine, Mr. Laverton-West. They aren't personal, you know."

The reply seemed to soothe the irate M.P.

"If that is all—"

"That is all for the present, Mr. Laverton-West."

"You will keep me informed—"

"Naturally, sir. By the way, let me introduce M. Hercule Poirot. You may have heard of him."

Mr. Laverton-West's eye fastened itself interestedly on the little Belgian.

"Yes—yes—I have heard the name."

"Monsieur," said Poirot, his manner suddenly very foreign. "Believe me, my heart bleeds for you. Such a loss! Such agony as you must be enduring! Ah, but I will say no more. How magnificently the English hide their emotions." He whipped out his cigarette case. "Permit me—Ah, it is empty. Japp?"

Japp slapped his pockets and shook his head.

Laverton-West produced his own cigarette case, murmured, "Er—have one of mine, M. Poirot."

"Thank you—thank you." The little man helped himself.

"As you say, M. Poirot," resumed the other, "we English do not parade our emotions. A stiff upper lip—that is our motto."

He bowed to the two men and went out.

"Bit of a stuffed fish," said Japp disgustedly. "And a boiled owl! The Plenderleith girl was quite right about him. Yet he's a good-looking sort of chap—might go down well with some woman who had no sense of humour. What about that cigarette?"

Poirot handed it over, shaking his head.

"Egyptian. An expensive variety."

"No, that's no good. A pity, for I've never heard a weaker alibi! In fact, it wasn't an alibi at all . . . You know, Poirot, it's a pity the boot wasn't on the other leg. If she'd been blackmailing him . . . He's a lovely type for blackmail—would pay out like a lamb! Anything to avoid a scandal."

"My friend, it is very pretty to reconstruct the case as you would like it to be, but that is not strictly our affair."

"No, Eustace is our affair. I've got a few lines on him. Definitely a nasty fellow."

"By the way, did you do as I suggested about Miss Plenderleith?"

"Yes. Wait a sec, I'll ring through and get the latest."

He picked up the telephone receiver and spoke through it.

After a brief interchange he replaced it and looked up at Poirot.

"Pretty heartless piece of goods. Gone off to play golf. That's a nice thing to do when your friend's been murdered only the day before."

Poirot uttered an exclamation.

"What's the matter now?" asked Japp.

But Poirot was murmuring to himself.

"Of course . . . of course . . . but naturally . . . What an imbecile I am—why, it leapt to the eye!"

Japp said rudely:

"Stop jabbering to yourself and let's go and tackle Eustace."

He was amazed to see the radiant smile that spread over Poirot's face.

"But—yes—most certainly let us tackle him. For now, see you, I know everything—but everything!"

<h1 style="text-align:center">XI</h1>

Major Eustace received the two men with the easy assurance of a man of the world.

His flat was small, a mere pied à terre, as he explained. He offered the two men a drink and when that was refused he took out his cigarette case.

Both Japp and Poirot accepted a cigarette. A quick glance passed between them.

"You smoke Turkish, I see," said Japp as he twirled the cigarette between his fingers.

"Yes. I'm sorry, do you prefer a gasper? I've got one somewhere about."

"No, no, this will do me very well." Then he leaned forward—his tone changed. "Perhaps you can guess, Major Eustace, what it was I came to see you about?"

The other shook his head. His manner was nonchalant. Major Eustace was a tall man, good-looking in a somewhat coarse fashion. There was a puffiness round the eyes—small, crafty eyes that belied the good-humoured geniality of his manner.

He said:

"No—I've no idea what brings such a big gun as a chief inspector to see me. Anything to do with my car?"

"No, it is not your car. I think you knew a Mrs. Barbara Allen, Major Eustace?"

The major leant back, puffed out a cloud of smoke, and said in an enlightened voice:

"Oh, so that's it! Of course, I might have guessed. Very sad business."

"You know about it?"

"Saw it in the paper last night. Too bad."

"You knew Mrs. Allen out in India, I think."

"Yes, that's some years ago now."

"Did you also know her husband?"

There was a pause—a mere fraction of a second—but during that fraction the little pig eyes flashed a quick look at the faces of the two men. Then he answered:

"No, as a matter of fact, I never came across Allen."

"But you know something about him?"

"Heard he was by way of being a bad hat. Of course, that was only rumour."

"Mrs. Allen did not say anything?"

"Never talked about him."

"You were on intimate terms with her?"

Major Eustace shrugged his shoulders.

"We were old friends, you know, old friends. But we didn't see each other very often."

"But you did see her that last evening? The evening of November fifth?"

"Yes, as a matter of fact, I did."

"You called at her house, I think."

Major Eustace nodded. His voice took on a gentle, regretful note.

"Yes, she asked me to advise her about some investments. Of course, I can see what you're driving at—her state of mind—all that sort of thing. Well, really, it's very difficult to say. Her manner seemed normal enough and yet she was a bit jumpy, come to think of it."

"But she gave you no hint as to what she contemplated doing?"

"Not the least in the world. As a matter of fact, when I said goodbye I said I'd ring her up soon and we'd do a show together."

"You said you'd ring her up. Those were your last words?"

"Yes."

"Curious. I have information that you said something quite different."

Eustace changed colour.

"Well, of course, I can't remember the exact words."

"My information is that what you actually said was, 'Well, think it over and let me know.' "

"Let me see, yes I believe you're right. Not exactly that. I think I was suggesting she should let me know when she was free."

"Not quite the same thing, is it?" said Japp.

Major Eustace shrugged his shoulders.

			The Plymouth Express Affair & Other Stories

"My dear fellow, you can't expect a man to remember word for word what he said on any given occasion."

"And what did Mrs. Allen reply?"

"She said she'd give me a ring. That is, as near as I can remember."

"And then you said, 'All right. So long.' "

"Probably. Something of the kind anyway."

Japp said quietly:

"You say that Mrs. Allen asked you to advise her about her investments. Did she, by any chance, entrust you with the sum of two hundred pounds in cash to invest for her?"

Eustace's face flushed a dark purple. He leaned forward and growled out:

"What the devil do you mean by that?"

"Did she or did she not?"

"That's my business, Mr. Chief Inspector."

Japp said quietly:

"Mrs. Allen drew out the sum of two hundred pounds in cash from her bank. Some of the money was in five-pound notes. The numbers of these can, of course, be traced."

"What if she did?"

"Was the money for investment—or was it—blackmail, Major Eustace?"

"That's a preposterous idea. What next will you suggest?"

Japp said in his most official manner:

"I think, Major Eustace, that at this point I must ask you if you are willing to come to Scotland Yard and make a statement. There is, of course, no compulsion and you can, if you prefer it, have your solicitor present."

"Solicitor? What the devil should I want with a solicitor? And what are you cautioning me for?"

"I am inquiring into the circumstances of the death of Mrs. Allen."

"Good God, man, you don't suppose—Why, that's nonsense! Look here, what happened was this. I called round to see Barbara by appointment. . . ."

"That was at what time?"

"At about half past nine, I should say. We sat and talked. . . ."

"And smoked?"

"Yes, and smoked. Anything damaging in that?" demanded the major belligerently.

"Where did this conversation take place?"

"In the sitting room. Left of the door as you go in. We talked together quite amicably, as I say. I left a little before half past ten. I stayed for a minute on the doorstep for a few last words. . . ."

"Last words—precisely," murmured Poirot.

"Who are you, I'd like to know?" Eustace turned and spart the words at him. "Some kind of damned dago! What are you butting in for?"

"I am Hercule Poirot," said the little man with dignity.

"I don't care if you are the Achilles statue. As I say, Barbara and I parted quite amicably. I drove straight to the Far East Club. Got there at five and twenty to eleven and went straight up to the card-room. Stayed there playing bridge until one thirty. Now then, put that in your pipe and smoke it."

"I do not smoke the pipe," said Poirot. "It is a pretty alibi you have there."

"It should be a pretty cast iron one anyway! Now then, sir," he looked at Japp. "Are you satisfied?"

"You remained in the sitting room throughout your visit?"

"Yes."

"You did not go upstairs to Mrs. Allen's own boudoir?"

"No, I tell you. We stayed in the one room and didn't leave it."

Japp looked at him thoughtfully for a minute or two. Then he said:

"How many sets of cuff links have you?"

"Cuff links? Cuff links? What's that got to do with it?"

"You are not bound to answer the question, of course."

"Answer it? I don't mind answering it. I've got nothing to hide. And I shall demand an apology. There are these . . ." he stretched out his arms.

Japp noted the gold and platinum with a nod.

"And I've got these."

He rose, opened a drawer and taking out a case, he opened it and shoved it rudely almost under Japp's nose.

"Very nice design," said the chief inspector. "I see one is broken—bit of enamel chipped off."

"What of it?"

"You don't remember when that happened, I suppose?"

"A day or two ago, not longer."

"Would you be surprised to hear that it happened when you were visiting Mrs. Allen?"

"Why shouldn't it? I've not denied that I was there." The major spoke haughtily. He continued to bluster, to act the part of the justly indignant man, but his hands were trembling.

Japp leaned forward and said with emphasis:

"Yes, but that bit of cuff link wasn't found in the sitting room. It was found upstairs in Mrs. Allen's boudoir—there in the room where she was killed, and where a man sat smoking the same kind of cigarettes as you smoke."

The shot told. Eustace fell back into his chair. His eyes went from side to side. The collapse of the bully and the appearance of the craven was not a pretty sight.

"You've got nothing on me." His voice was almost a whine. "You're trying to frame me . . . But you can't do it. I've got an alibi . . . I never came near the house again that night. . . ."

Poirot in his turn, spoke.

"No, you did not come near the house again . . . You did not need to . . . For perhaps Mrs. Allen was already dead when you left it."

"That's impossible—impossible—She was just inside the door—she spoke to me—People must have heard her—seen her. . . ."

Poirot said softly:

"They heard you speaking to her . . . and pretending to wait for her answer and then speaking again . . . It is an old trick that . . . People may have assumed she was there, but they did not see her, because they could not even say whether she was wearing evening dress or not—not even mention what colour she was wearing. . . ."

"My God—it isn't true—it isn't true—"

He was shaking now—collapsed. . . .

Japp looked at him with disgust. He spoke crisply.

"I'll have to ask you, sir, to come with me."

"You're arresting me?"

"Detained for inquiry—we'll put it that way."

The silence was broken with a long, shuddering sigh. The despairing voice of the erstwhile blustering Major Eustace said:

"I'm sunk. . . ."

Hercule Poirot rubbed his hands together and smiled cheerfully. He seemed to be enjoying himself.

XII

"Pretty the way he went all to pieces," said Japp with professional appreciation, later that day.

He and Poirot were driving in a car along the Brompton Road.

"He knew the game was up," said Poirot absently.

"We've got plenty on him," said Japp. "Two or three different aliases, a tricky business over a cheque, and a very nice affair when he stayed at the Ritz and called himself Colonel de Bathe. Swindled half a dozen Piccadilly tradesmen. We're holding him on that charge for the moment—until we get this affair finally squared up. What's the idea of this rush to the country, old man?"

"My friend, an affair must be rounded off properly. Everything must be explained. I am on the quest of the mystery you suggested. The Mystery of the Missing Attaché Case."

"The Mystery of the Small Attaché Case—that's what I called it—It isn't missing that I know of."

"Wait, mon ami."

The car turned into the mews. At the door of No. 14, Jane Plenderleith was just alighting from a small Austin Seven. She was in golfing clothes.

She looked from one to the other of the two men, then produced a key and opened the door.

"Come in, won't you?"

She led the way. Japp followed her into the sitting room. Poirot remained for a minute or two in the hall, muttering something about:

"C'est embêtant—how difficult to get out of these sleeves."

In a moment or two he also entered the sitting room minus his overcoat but Japp's lips twitched under his moustache. He had heard the very faint squeak of an opening cupboard door.

Japp threw Poirot an inquiring glance and the other gave a hardly perceptible nod.

"We won't detain you, Miss Plenderleith," said Japp briskly.

"Only came to ask if you could tell us the name of Mrs. Allen's solicitor."

"Her solicitor?" The girl shook her head. "I don't even know that she had one."

"Well, when she rented this house with you, someone must have drawn up the agreement?"

"No, I don't think so. You see, I took the house, the lease is in my name. Barbara paid me half the rent. It was quite informal."

"I see. Oh! well, I suppose there's nothing doing then."

"I'm sorry I can't help you," said Jane politely.

"It doesn't really matter very much." Japp turned towards the door. "Been playing golf?"

"Yes." She flushed. "I suppose it seems rather heartless to you. But as a matter of fact it got me down rather, being here in this house. I felt I must go out and do something—tire myself—or I'd choke!"

She spoke with intensity.

Poirot said quickly:

"I comprehend, mademoiselle. It is most understandable—most natural. To sit in this house and think—no, it would not be pleasant."

"So long as you understand," said Jane shortly.

"You belong to a club?"

"Yes, I play at Wentworth."

"It has been a pleasant day," said Poirot.

"Alas, there are few leaves left on the trees now! A week ago the woods were magnificent."

"It was quite lovely today."

"Good afternoon, Miss Plenderleith," said Japp formally. "I'll let you know when there's anything definite. As a matter of fact we have got a man detained on suspicion."

"What man?"

She looked at them eagerly.

"Major Eustace."

She nodded and turned away, stooping down to put a match to the fire.

"Well?" said Japp as the car turned the corner of the mews.

Poirot grinned.

"It was quite simple. The key was in the door this time."

"And—?"

Poirot smiled.

"Eh, bien, the golf clubs had gone—"

"Naturally. The girl isn't a fool, whatever else she is. Anything else gone?"

Poirot nodded his head.

"Yes, my friend—the little attaché case!"

The accelerator leaped under Japp's foot.

"Damnation!" he said. "I knew there was something. But what the devil is it? I searched that case pretty thoroughly."

"My poor Japp—but it is—how do you say, 'obvious, my dear Watson?' "

Japp threw him an exasperated look.

"Where are we going?" he asked.

Poirot consulted his watch.

"It is not yet four o'clock. We could get to Wentworth, I think, before it is dark."

"Do you think she really went there?"

"I think so—yes. She would know that we might make inquiries. Oh, yes, I think we will find that she has been there."

Japp grunted.

"Oh well, come on." He threaded his way dexterously through the traffic. "Though what this attaché case business has to do with the crime I can't imagine. I can't see that it's got anything at all to do with it."

"Precisely, my friend, I agree with you—it has nothing to do with it."

"Then why—No, don't tell me! Order and method and everything nicely rounded off! Oh, well, it's a fine day."

The car was a fast one. They arrived at Wentworth Golf Club a little after half past four. There was no great congestion there on a week day.

Poirot went straight to the caddie-master and asked for Miss Plenderleith's clubs. She would be playing on a different course tomorrow, he explained.

The caddie master raised his voice and a boy sorted through some golf clubs standing in a corner. He finally produced a bag bearing the initials, J.P.

"Thank you," said Poirot. He moved away, then turned carelessly and asked, "She did not leave with you a small attaché case also, did she?"

"Not today, sir. May have left it in the clubhouse."

"She was down here today?"

"Oh, yes, I saw her."

"Which caddie did she have, do you know? She's mislaid an attaché case and can't remember where she had it last."

"She didn't take a caddie. She came in here and bought a couple of balls. Just took out a couple of irons. I rather fancy she had a little case in her hand then."

Poirot turned away with a word of thanks. The two men walked round the clubhouse. Poirot stood a moment admiring the view.

"It is beautiful, is it not, the dark pine trees—and then the lake. Yes, the lake—"

Japp gave him a quick glance.

"That's the idea, is it?"

Poirot smiled.

"I think it possible that someone may have seen something. I should set the inquiries in motion if I were you."

XIII

Poirot stepped back, his head a little on one side as he surveyed the arrangement of the room. A chair here—another chair there. Yes, that was very nice. And now a ring at the bell—that would be Japp.

The Scotland Yard man came in alertly.

"Quite right, old cock! Straight from the horse's mouth. A young woman was seen to throw something into the lake at Wentworth yesterday. Description of her answers to Jane Plenderleith. We managed to fish it up without much difficulty. A lot of reeds just there."

"And it was?"

"It was the attaché case all right! But why, in heaven's name? Well, it beats me! Nothing inside it—not even the magazines. Why a presumably sane young woman should want to fling an expensively-fitted dressing case into a lake—d'you know, I worried all night because I couldn't get the hang of it."

"Mon pauvre Japp! But you need worry no longer. Here is the answer coming. The bell has just rung."

Georges, Poirot's immaculate manservant, opened the door and announced:

"Miss Plenderleith."

The girl came into the room with her usual air of complete self-assurance. She greeted the two men.

"I asked you to come here—" explained Poirot. "Sit here, will you not, and you here, Japp—because I have certain news to give you."

The girl sat down. She looked from one to the other, pushing aside her hat. She took it off and laid it aside impatiently.

"Well," she said. "Major Eustace has been arrested."

"You saw that, I expect, in the morning paper?"

"Yes."

"He is at the moment charged with a minor offence," went on Poirot. "In the meantime we are gathering evidence in connection with the murder."

"It was murder, then?"

The girl asked it eagerly.

Poirot nodded his head.

"Yes," he said. "It was murder. The wilful destruction of one human being by another human being."

She shivered a little.

"Don't," she murmured. "It sounds horrible when you say it like that."

"Yes—but it is horrible!"

He paused—then he said:

"Now, Miss Plenderleith, I am going to tell you just how I arrived at the truth in this matter."

She looked from Poirot to Japp. The latter was smiling.

"He has his methods, Miss Plenderleith," he said. "I humour him, you know. I think we'll listen to what he has to say."

Poirot began:

"As you know, mademoiselle, I arrived with my friend at the scene of the crime on the morning of November the sixth. We went into the room where the body of Mrs. Allen had been found and I was struck at once by several significant details. There were things, you see, in that room that were decidedly odd."

"Go on," said the girl.

"To begin with," said Poirot, "there was the smell of cigarette smoke."

"I think you're exaggerating there, Poirot," said Japp. "I didn't smell anything."

Poirot turned on him in a flash.

"Precisely. You did not smell any stale smoke. No more did I. And that was very, very strange—for the door and the window were both closed and on an ashtray there were the stubs of no fewer than ten cigarettes. It was odd, very odd, that the room should smell—as it did, perfectly fresh."

"So that's what you were getting at!" Japp sighed. "Always have to get at things in such a tortuous way."

"Your Sherlock Holmes did the same. He drew attention, remember, to the curious incident of the dog in the nighttime—and the answer to that was there was no curious incident. The dog did nothing in the nighttime. To proceed:

"The next thing that attracted my attention was a wristwatch worn by the dead woman."

"What about it?"

"Nothing particular about it, but it was worn on the right wrist. Now in my experience it is more usual for a watch to be worn on the left wrist."

Japp shrugged his shoulders. Before he could speak, Poirot hurried on:

"But as you say, there is nothing very definite about that. Some people prefer to wear one on the right hand. And now I come to something really interesting—I come, my friends, to the writing bureau."

"Yes, I guessed that," said Japp.

"That was really very odd—very remarkable! For two reasons. The first reason was that something was missing from that writing table."

Jane Plenderleith spoke.

"What was missing?"

Poirot turned to her.

"A sheet of blotting paper, mademoiselle. The blotting book had on top a clean, untouched piece of blotting paper."

Jane shrugged her shoulders.

"Really, M. Poirot. People do occasionally tear off a very much used sheet!"

"Yes, but what do they do with it? Throw it into the wastepaper basket, do they not? But it was not in the wastepaper basket. I looked."

Jane Plenderleith seemed impatient.

"Because it had probably been already thrown away the day before. The sheet was clean because Barbara hadn't written any letters that day."

"That could hardly be the case, mademoiselle. For Mrs. Allen was seen going to the postbox that evening. Therefore she must have been writing letters. She could not write downstairs—there were no writing materials. She would be hardly likely to go to your room to write. So, then, what had happened to the sheet of paper on which she had blotted her letters? It is true that people sometimes throw things in the fire instead of the wastepaper basket, but there was only a gas fire in the room. And the fire downstairs had not been alight the previous day, since you told me it was all laid ready when you put a match to it."

He paused.

"A curious little problem. I looked everywhere, in the wastepaper baskets, in the dustbin, but I could not find a sheet of used blotting paper—and that seemed to me very important. It looked as though someone had deliberately taken that sheet of blotting paper away. Why? Because there was writing on it that could easily have been read by holding it up to a mirror.

"But there was a second curious point about the writing table. Perhaps, Japp, you remember roughly the arrangement of it? Blotter and inkstand in the centre, pen tray to the left, calendar and quill pen to the right. Eh bien? You do not see? The quill pen, remember,

I examined, it was for show only—it had not been used. Ah! still you do not see? I will say it again. Blotter in the centre, pen tray to the left—to the left, Japp. But is it not usual to find a pen tray on the right, convenient to the right hand?

"Ah, now it comes to you, does it not? The pen tray on the left—the wristwatch on the right wrist—the blotting paper removed—and something else brought into the room—the ashtray with the cigarette ends!

"That room was fresh and pure smelling, Japp, a room in which the window had been open, not closed all night . . . And I made myself a picture."

He spun round and faced Jane.

"A picture of you, mademoiselle, driving up in your taxi, paying it off, running up the stairs, calling perhaps, 'Barbara'—and you open the door and you find your friend there lying dead with the pistol clasped in her hand—the left hand, naturally, since she is left-handed and therefore, too, the bullet has entered on the left side of the head. There is a note there addressed to you. It tells you what it is that has driven her to take her own life. It was, I fancy, a very moving letter . . . A young, gentle, unhappy woman driven by blackmail to take her life. . . .

"I think that, almost at once, the idea flashed into your head. This was a certain man's doing. Let him be punished—fully and adequately punished! You take the pistol, wipe it and place it in the right hand. You take the note and you tear off the top sheet of the blotting paper on which the note has been blotted. You go down, light the fire and put them both on the flames. Then you carry up the ashtray—to further the illusion that two people sat there talking—and you also take up a fragment of enamel cuff link that is on the floor. That is a lucky find and you expect it to clinch matters. Then you close the window and lock the door. There must be no suspicion that you have tampered with the room. The police must see it exactly as it is—so you do not seek help in the mews but ring up the police straightaway.

"And so it goes on. You play your chosen rôle with judgment and coolness. You refuse at first to say anything but cleverly you suggest doubts of suicide. Later you are quite ready to set us on the trail of Major Eustace. . . .

"Yes, mademoiselle, it was clever—a very clever murder—for that is what it is. The attempted murder of Major Eustace."

Jane Plenderleith sprang to her feet.

"It wasn't murder—it was justice. That man hounded poor Barbara to her death! She was so sweet and helpless. You see, poor kid, she got involved with a man in India when she first went out. She was only seventeen and he was a married man years older than her. Then she had a baby. She could have put it in a home but she wouldn't hear of that. She went off to some out of the way spot and came back calling herself Mrs. Allen. Later the child died. She came back here and she fell in love with Charles—that pompous, stuffed owl; she adored him—and he took her adoration very complacently. If he had been a different kind of man I'd have advised her to tell him everything. But as it was, I urged her to hold her tongue. After all, nobody knew anything about that business except me.

"And then that devil Eustace turned up! You know the rest. He began to bleed her systematically, but it wasn't till that last evening that she realised that she was exposing Charles too, to the risk of scandal. Once married to Charles, Eustace had got her where he wanted her— married to a rich man with a horror of any scandal! When Eustace had gone with the money she had got for him she sat thinking it over. Then she came up and wrote a letter to me. She said she loved Charles and couldn't live without him, but that for his own sake she mustn't marry him. She was taking the best way out, she said."

Jane flung her head back.

"Do you wonder I did what I did? And you stand there calling it murder!"

"Because it is murder," Poirot's voice was stern. "Murder can sometimes seem justified, but it is murder all the same. You are truthful and clear-minded—face the truth, mademoiselle! Your friend died, in the last resort, because she had not the courage to live. We may sympathize with her. We may pity her. But the fact remains—the act was hers—not another."

He paused.

"And you? That man is now in prison, he will serve a long sentence for other matters. Do you really wish, of your own volition, to destroy the life—the life, mind—of any human being?"

She stared at him. Her eyes darkened. Suddenly she muttered:

"No. You're right. I don't."

Then, turning on her heel, she went swiftly from the room. The outer door banged. . . .

XIV

Japp gave a long—a very prolonged—whistle.

"Well, I'm damned!" he said.

Poirot sat down and smiled at him amiably. It was quite a long time before the silence was broken. Then Japp said:

"Not murder disguised as suicide, but suicide made to look like murder!"

"Yes, and very cleverly done, too. Nothing overemphasized."

Japp said suddenly:

"But the attaché case? Where did that come in?"

"But, my dear, my very dear friend, I have already told you that it did not come in."

"Then why—"

"The golf clubs. The golf clubs, Japp. They were the golf clubs of a left-handed person. Jane Plenderleith kept her clubs at Wentworth. Those were Barbara Allen's clubs. No wonder the girl got, as you say, the wind up when we opened that cupboard. Her whole plan might have been ruined. But she is quick, she realized that she had, for one short moment, given herself away. She saw that we saw. So she does the best thing she can think of on the spur of the moment. She tries to focus our attention on the wrong object. She says of the attaché case 'That's mine. I—it came back with me this morning. So there can't be anything there.' And, as she hoped, away you go on the false trail. For the same reason, when she sets out the following day to get rid of the golf clubs, she continues to use the attaché case as a—what is it—kippered herring?"

"Red herring. Do you mean that her real object was—?"

"Consider, my friend. Where is the best place to get rid of a bag of golf clubs? One cannot burn them or put them in a dustbin. If one leaves them somewhere they may be returned to you. Miss Plenderleith took them to a golf course. She leaves them in the clubhouse while she gets a couple of irons from her own bag, and then she goes round without a caddy. Doubtless at judicious intervals she breaks a club in half and throws it into some deep undergrowth, and ends by throwing the empty bag away. If anyone should find a broken golf club here and there it will not create surprise. People have been known to break and throw away all their clubs in a mood of intense exasperation over the game! It is, in fact, that kind of game!

"But since she realizes that her actions may still be a matter of interest, she throws that useful red herring—the attaché case—in a somewhat spectacular manner into the lake—and that, my friend, is the truth of 'The Mystery of the Attaché Case.' "

Japp looked at his friend for some moments in silence. Then he rose, clapped him on the shoulder, and burst out laughing.

"Not so bad for an old dog! Upon my word, you take the cake! Come out and have a spot of lunch?"

"With pleasure, my friend, but we will not have the cake. Indeed, an Omelette aux Champignons, Blanquette de Veau, Petits pois à la Francaise, and—to follow—a Baba au Rhum."

"Lead me to it," said Japp.

                    The Plymouth Express Affair & Other Stories

The Nemean Lion

"Anything of interest this morning, Miss Lemon?" he asked as he entered the room the following morning.

He trusted Miss Lemon. She was a woman without imagination, but she had an instinct. Anything that she mentioned as worth consideration usually was worth consideration. She was a born secretary.

"Nothing much, M. Poirot. There is just one letter that I thought might interest you. I have put it on the top of the pile."

"And what is that?" He took an interested step forward.

"It's from a man who wants you to investigate the disappearance of his wife's Pekinese dog."

Poirot paused with his foot still in the air. He threw a glance of deep reproach at Miss Lemon. She did not notice it. She had begun to type. She typed with the speed and precision of a quick-firing tank.

Poirot was shaken; shaken and embittered. Miss Lemon, the efficient Miss Lemon, had let him down! A Pekinese dog. A Pekinese dog! And after the dream he had had last night. He had been leaving Buckingham Palace after being personally thanked when his valet had come in with his morning chocolate!

Words trembled on his lips—witty caustic words. He did not utter them because Miss Lemon, owing to the speed and efficiency of her typing, would not have heard them.

With a grunt of disgust he picked up the topmost letter from the little pile on the side of his desk.

Yes, it was exactly as Miss Lemon had said. A city address—a curt businesslike unrefined demand. The subject—the kidnapping of a Pekinese dog. One of those bulging-eyed, overpampered pets of a rich woman. Hercule Poirot's lip curled as he read it.

Nothing unusual about this. Nothing out of the way or—But yes, yes, in one small detail, Miss Lemon was right. In one small detail there was something unusual.

Hercule Poirot sat down. He read the letter slowly and carefully. It was not the kind of case he wanted, it was not the kind of case he had promised himself. It was not in any sense an important case, it was supremely unimportant. It was not—and here was the crux of his objection—it was not a proper Labor of Hercules.

But unfortunately he was curious. . . .

Yes, he was curious. . . .

He raised his voice so as to be heard by Miss Lemon above the noise of her typing.

"Ring up this Sir Joseph Hoggin," he ordered, "and make an appointment for me to see him at his office as he suggests."

As usual, Miss Lemon had been right.

"I'm a plain man, Mr. Poirot," said Sir Joseph Hoggin.

Hercule Poirot made a noncommittal gesture with his right hand. It expressed (if you chose to take it so) admiration for the solid worth of Sir Joseph's career and an appreciation of his modesty in so describing himself. It could also have conveyed a graceful deprecation of the statement. In any case it gave no clue to the thought then uppermost in Hercule Poirot's mind, which was that Sir Joseph certainly was (using the term in its more colloquial sense) a very plain man indeed. Hercule Poirot's eyes rested critically on the swelling jowl, the small pig eyes, the bulbous nose and the close-lipped mouth. The whole general effect reminded him of someone or something—but for the moment he could not recollect who or what it was. A memory stirred dimly. A long time ago . . . in Belgium . . . something, surely, to do with soap. . . .

Sir Joseph was continuing.

"No frills about me. I don't beat about the bush. Most people, Mr. Poirot, would let this business go. Write it off as a bad debt and forget about it. But that's not Joseph Hoggin's way. I'm a rich man—and in a manner of speaking two hundred pounds is neither here nor there to me—"

Poirot interpolated swiftly:

"I congratulate you."

"Eh?"

Sir Joseph paused a minute. His small eyes narrowed themselves still more. He said sharply:

"That's not to say that I'm in the habit of throwing my money about. What I want I pay for. But I pay the market price—no more."

Hercule Poirot said:

"You realize that my fees are high?"

"Yes, yes. But this," Sir Joseph looked at him cunningly, "is a very small matter."

Hercule Poirot shrugged his shoulders. He said:

"I do not bargain. I am an expert. For the services of an expert you have to pay."

Sir Joseph said frankly:

"I know you're a tip-top man at this sort of thing. I made inquiries and I was told that you were the best man available. I mean to get to the bottom of this business and I don't grudge the expense. That's why I got you to come here."

"You were fortunate," said Hercule Poirot.

Sir Joseph said "Eh?" again.

"Exceedingly fortunate," said Hercule Poirot firmly. "I am, I may say so without undue modesty, at the apex of my career. Very shortly I intend to retire—to live in the country, to travel occasionally to see the world—also, it may be, to cultivate my garden—with particular attention to improving the strain of vegetable marrows. Magnificent vegetables—but they lack flavour. That, however, is not the point. I wished merely to explain that before retiring I had imposed upon myself a certain task. I have decided to accept twelve cases—no more, no less. A self-imposed 'Labors of Hercules' if I may so describe it. Your case, Sir Joseph, is the first of the twelve. I was attracted to it," he sighed, "by its striking unimportance."

"Importance?" said Sir Joseph.

"Unimportance was what I said. I have been called in for varying causes—to investigate murders, unexplained deaths, robberies, thefts of jewellery. This is the first time that I have been asked to turn my talents to elucidate the kidnapping of a Pekinese dog."

Sir Joseph grunted. He said:

"You surprise me! I should have said you'd have had no end of women pestering you about their pet dogs."

"That, certainly. But it is the first time that I am summoned by the husband in the case."

Sir Joseph's little eyes narrowed appreciatively.

He said:

"I begin to see why they recommended you to me. You're a shrewd fellow, Mr. Poirot."

Poirot murmured:

"If you will now tell me the facts of the case. The dog disappeared, when?"

"Exactly a week ago."

"And your wife is by now quite frantic, I presume?"

Sir Joseph stared. He said:

"You don't understand. The dog has been returned."

"Returned? Then, permit me to ask, where do I enter the matter?"

Sir Joseph went crimson in the face.

"Because I'm damned if I'll be swindled! Now then, Mr. Poirot, I'm going to tell you the whole thing. The dog was stolen a week ago—nipped in Kensington Gardens where he was out with my wife's companion. The next day my wife got a demand for two hundred pounds. I ask you—two hundred pounds! For a damned yapping little brute that's always getting under your feet anyway!"

Poirot murmured:

"You did not approve of paying such a sum, naturally?"

"Of course I didn't—or wouldn't have if I'd known anything about it! Milly (my wife) knew that well enough. She didn't say anything to me. Just sent off the money—in one pound notes as stipulated—to the address given."

"And the dog was returned?"

"Yes. That evening the bell rang and there was the little brute sitting on the doorstep. And not a soul to be seen."

"Perfectly. Continue."

"Then, of course, Milly confessed what she'd done and I lost my temper a bit. However, I calmed down after a while—after all, the thing was done and you can't expect a woman to behave with any sense—and I daresay I should have let the whole thing go if it hadn't been for meeting old Samuelson at the Club."

"Yes?"

"Damn it all, this thing must be a positive racket! Exactly the same thing had happened to him. Three hundred pounds they'd rooked his wife of! Well, that was a bit too much. I decided the thing had got to be stopped. I sent for you."

"But surely, Sir Joseph, the proper thing (and a very much more inexpensive thing) would have been to send for the police?"

Sir Joseph rubbed his nose.

He said:

"Are you married, Mr. Poirot?"

"Alas," said Poirot, "I have not that felicity."

"H'm," said Sir Joseph. "Don't know about felicity, but if you were, you'd know that women are funny creatures. My wife went into hysterics at the mere mention of the police—she'd got it into her head that something would happen to her precious Shan Tung if I went to them. She wouldn't hear of the idea—and I may say she doesn't take very kindly to the idea of your being called in. But I stood firm there and at last she gave way. But, mind you, she doesn't like it."

Hercule Poirot murmured:

"The position is, I perceive, a delicate one. It would be as well, perhaps, if I were to interview Madame your wife and gain further particulars from her whilst at the same time reassuring her as to the future safety of her dog?"

Sir Joseph nodded and rose to his feet. He said:

"I'll take you along in the car right away."

II

In a large, hot, ornately furnished drawing room two women were sitting.

As Sir Joseph and Hercule Poirot entered, a small Pekinese dog rushed forward, barking furiously, and circling dangerously round Poirot's ankles.

"Shan—Shan, come here. Come here to mother, lovey—Pick him up, Miss Carnaby."

The second woman hurried forward and Hercule Poirot murmured:

"A veritable lion, indeed."

Rather breathlessly Shan Tung's captor agreed.

"Yes, indeed, he's such a good watch dog. He's not frightened of anything or any one. There's a lovely boy, then."

Having performed the necessary introduction, Sir Joseph said:

"Well, Mr. Poirot, I'll leave you to get on with it," and with a short nod he left the room.

Lady Hoggin was a stout, petulant-looking woman with dyed henna red hair. Her companion, the fluttering Miss Carnaby, was a plump, amiable-looking creature between forty and fifty. She treated Lady Hoggin with great deference and was clearly frightened to death of her.

Poirot said:

"Now tell me, Lady Hoggin, the full circumstances of this abominable crime."

Lady Hoggin flushed.

"I'm very glad to hear you say that, Mr. Poirot. For it was a crime. Pekinese are terribly sensitive—just as sensitive as children. Poor Shan Tung might have died of fright if of nothing else."

Miss Carnaby chimed in breathlessly:

"Yes, it was wicked—wicked!"

"Please tell me the facts."

"Well, it was like this. Shan Tung was out for his walk in the Park with Miss Carnaby—"

"Oh dear me, yes, it was all my fault," chimed in the companion. "How could I have been so stupid—so careless—"

Lady Hoggin said acidly:

"I don't want to reproach you, Miss Carnaby, but I do think you might have been more alert."

Poirot transferred his gaze to the companion.

"What happened?"

Miss Carnaby burst into voluble and slightly flustered speech.

"Well, it was the most extraordinary thing! We had just been along the flower walk—Shan Tung was on the lead, of course—he'd had his little run on the grass—and I was just about to turn and go home when my attention was caught by a baby in a pram—such a lovely baby—it smiled at me—lovely rosy cheeks and such curls. I couldn't just resist speaking to the nurse in charge and asking how old it was—seventeen months, she said—and I'm sure I was only speaking to her for about a minute or two, and then suddenly I looked down and Shan wasn't there any more. The lead had been cut right through—"

Lady Hoggin said:

"If you'd been paying proper attention to your duties, nobody could have sneaked up and cut that lead."

Miss Carnaby seemed inclined to burst into tears. Poirot said hastily:

"And what happened next?"

"Well, of course I looked everywhere. And called! And I asked the Park attendant if he'd seen a man carrying a Pekinese dog but he hadn't noticed anything of the kind—and I didn't know what to do—and I went on searching, but at last, of course, I had to come home—"

Miss Carnaby stopped dead. Poirot could imagine the scene that followed well enough. He asked:

"And then you received a letter?"

Lady Hoggin took up the tale.

"By the first post the following morning. It said that if I wanted to see Shan Tung alive I was to send £200 in one pound notes in an unregistered packet to Captain Curtis, 38 Bloomsbury Road Square. It said that if the money were marked or the police informed then—then—Shan Tung's ears and tail would be—cut off!"

Miss Carnaby began to sniff.

"So awful," she murmured. "How people can be such fiends!"

Lady Hoggin went on:

"It said that if I sent the money at once, Shan Tung would be returned the same evening alive and well, but that if—if afterwards I went to the police, it would be Shan Tung who would suffer for it—"

Miss Carnaby murmured tearfully:

"Oh dear, I'm so afraid that even now—of course, M. Poirot isn't exactly the police—"

Lady Hoggin said anxiously:

"So you see, Mr. Poirot, you will have to be very careful."

Hercule Poirot was quick to allay her anxiety.

"But I, I am not of the police. My inquiries, they will be conducted very discreetly, very quietly. You can be assured, Lady Hoggin, that Shan Tung will be perfectly safe. That I will guarantee."

Both ladies seemed relieved by the magic word. Poirot went on: "You have here the letter?"

Lady Hoggin shook her head.

"No, I was instructed to enclose it with the money."

"And you did so?"

"Yes."

"H'm, that is a pity."

Miss Carnaby said brightly:

"But I have the dog lead still. Shall I get it?"

She left the room. Hercule Poirot profited by her absence to ask a few pertinent questions.

"Amy Carnaby? Oh! she's quite all right. A good soul, though foolish, of course. I have had several companions and they have all been complete fools. But Amy was devoted to Shan Tung and she was terribly upset over the whole thing—as well she might be—hanging over perambulators and neglecting my little sweetheart! These old maids are all the same, idiotic over babies! No, I'm quite sure she had nothing whatever to do with it."

"It does not seem likely," Poirot agreed. "But as the dog disappeared when in her charge one must make quite certain of her honesty. She has been with you long?"

"Nearly a year. I had excellent references with her. She was with old Lady Hartingfield until she died—ten years, I believe. After that she looked after an invalid sister for a while. She really is an excellent creature—but a complete fool, as I said."

Amy Carnaby returned at this minute, slightly more out of breath, and produced the cut dog lead which she handed to Poirot with the utmost solemnity, looking at him with hopeful expectancy.

Poirot surveyed it carefully.

"Mais oui," he said. "This has undoubtedly been cut."

The two women waited expectantly. He said:

"I will keep this."

Solemnly he put it in his pocket. The two women breathed a sigh of relief. He had clearly done what was expected of him.

III

It was the habit of Hercule Poirot to leave nothing untested.

Though on the face of it it seemed unlikely that Miss Carnaby was anything but the foolish and rather muddle-headed woman that she appeared to be, Poirot nevertheless managed to interview a somewhat forbidding lady who was the niece of the late Lady Hartingfield.

"Amy Carnaby?" said Miss Maltravers. "Of course, remember her perfectly. She was a good soul and suited Aunt Julia down to the ground. Devoted to dogs and excellent at reading aloud. Tactful, too, never contradicted an invalid. What's happened to her? Not in distress of any kind, I hope. I gave her a reference about a year ago to some woman—name began with H—"

Poirot explained hastily that Miss Carnaby was still in her post. There had been, he said, a little trouble over a lost dog.

"Amy Carnaby is devoted to dogs. My aunt had a Pekinese. She left it to Miss Carnaby when she died and Miss Carnaby was devoted to it. I believe she was quite heartbroken when it died. Oh yes, she's a good soul. Not, of course, precisely intellectual."

Hercule Poirot agreed that Miss Carnaby could not, perhaps, be described as intellectual.

His next proceeding was to discover the Park Keeper to whom Miss Carnaby had spoken on the fateful afternoon. This he did without much difficulty. The man remembered the incident in question.

"Middle-aged lady, rather stout—in a regular state she was—lost her Pekinese dog. I knew her well by sight—brings the dog along most afternoons. I saw her come in with it. She was in a rare taking when she lost it. Came running to me to know if I'd seen any one with a Pekinese dog! Well, I ask you! I can tell you, the Gardens is full of dogs—every kind—terriers, Pekes, German sausage-dogs—even them Borzois—all kinds we have. Not likely as I'd notice one Peke more than another."

Hercule Poirot nodded his head thoughtfully.

He went to 38 Bloomsbury Road Square.

Nos. 38, 39 and 40 were incorporated together as the Balaclava Private Hotel. Poirot walked up the steps and pushed open the door. He was greeted inside by gloom and a smell of cooking cabbage with a reminiscence of breakfast kippers. On his left was a mahogany table with a sad-looking chrysanthemum plant on it. Above the table was a big baize-covered rack into which letters were stuck. Poirot stared at the board thoughtfully for some minutes. He pushed open a door on his right. It led into a kind of lounge with small tables and some so-called easy chairs covered with a depressing pattern of cretonne. Three old ladies and one fierce-looking old gentleman raised their heads and gazed at the intruder with deadly venom. Hercule Poirot blushed and withdrew.

He walked farther along the passage and came to a staircase. On his right a passage branched at right angles to what was evidently the dining room.

A little way along this passage was a door marked "Office."

On this Poirot tapped. Receiving no response, he opened the door and looked in. There was a large desk in the room covered with papers but there was no one to be seen. He withdrew, closing the door again. He penetrated to the dining room.

A sad-looking girl in a dirty apron was shuffling about with a basket of knives and forks with which she was laying the tables.

Hercule Poirot said apologetically:

"Excuse me, but could I see the Manageress?"

The girl looked at him with lacklustre eyes.

She said:

"I don't know, I'm sure."

Hercule Poirot said:

"There is no one in the office."

"Well, I don't know where she'd be, I'm sure."

"Perhaps," Hercule Poirot said, patient and persistent, "you could find out?"

The girl sighed. Dreary as her day's round was, it had now been made additionally so by this new burden laid upon her. She said sadly:

"Well, I'll see what I can do."

Poirot thanked her and removed himself once more to the hall, not daring to face the malevolent glare of the occupants of the lounge. He was staring up at the baize-covered letter rack when a rustle and a strong smell of Devonshire violets proclaimed the arrival of the Manageress.

Mrs. Harte was full of graciousness. She exclaimed:

"So sorry I was not in my office. You were requiring rooms?"

Hercule Poirot murmured:

"Not precisely. I was wondering if a friend of mine had been staying here lately. A Captain Curtis."

"Curtis," exclaimed Mrs. Harte. "Captain Curtis? Now where have I heard that name?"

Poirot did not help her. She shook her head vexedly.

He said:

"You have not, then, had a Captain Curtis staying here?"

"Well, not lately, certainly. And yet, you know, the name is certainly familiar to me. Can you describe your friend at all?"

"That," said Hercule Poirot, "would be difficult." He went on: "I suppose it sometimes happens that letters arrive for people when in actual fact no one of that name is staying here?"

"That does happen, of course."

"What do you do with such letters?"

"Well, we keep them for a time. You see, it probably means that the person in question will arrive shortly. Of course, if letters or parcels are a long time here unclaimed, they are returned to the post office."

Hercule Poirot nodded thoughtfully.

He said:

"I comprehend." He added: "It is like this, you see. I wrote a letter to my friend here."

Mrs. Harte's face cleared.

"That explains it. I must have noticed the name on an envelope. But really we have so many ex-Army gentlemen staying here or passing through—Let me see now."

She peered up at the board.

Hercule Poirot said:

"It is not there now."

"It must have been returned to the postman, I suppose. I am so sorry. Nothing important, I hope?"

"No, no, it was of no importance."

As he moved towards the door, Mrs. Harte, enveloped in her pungent odour of violets, pursued him.

"If your friend should come—"

"It is most unlikely. I must have made a mistake. . . ."

"Our terms," said Mrs. Harte, "are very moderate. Coffee after dinner is included. I would like you to see one or two of our bedsitting rooms. . . ."

With difficulty Hercule Poirot escaped.

IV

The drawing room of Mrs. Samuelson was larger, more lavishly furnished, and enjoyed an even more stifling amount of central heating than that of Lady Hoggin. Hercule Poirot picked his way giddily amongst gilded console tables and large groups of statuary.

Mrs. Samuelson was taller than Lady Hoggin and her hair was dyed with peroxide. Her Pekinese was called Nanki Poo. His bulging eyes surveyed Hercule Poirot with arrogance. Miss Keble, Mrs. Samuelson's companion, was thin and scraggy where Miss Carnaby had been plump, but she also was voluble and slightly breathless. She, too, had been blamed for Nanki Poo's disappearance.

"But really, Mr. Poirot, it was the most amazing thing. It all happened in a second. Outside Harrods it was. A nurse there asked me the time—"

Poirot interrupted her.

"A nurse? A hospital nurse?"

"No, no—a children's nurse. Such a sweet baby it was, too! A dear little mite. Such lovely rosy cheeks. They say children don't look healthy in London, but I'm sure—"

"Ellen," said Mrs. Samuelson.

Miss Keble blushed, stammered, and subsided into silence.

Mrs. Samuelson said acidly:

"And while Miss Keble was bending over a perambulator that had nothing to do with her, this audacious villain cut Nanki Poo's lead and made off with him."

Miss Keble murmured tearfully:

"It all happened in a second. I looked round and the darling boy was gone—there was just the dangling lead in my hand. Perhaps you'd like to see the lead, Mr. Poirot?"

"By no means," said Poirot hastily. He had no wish to make a collection of cut dog leads. "I understand," he went on, "that shortly afterwards you received a letter?"

The story followed the same course exactly—the letter—the threats of violence to Nanki Poo's ears and tail. Only two things were different—the sum of money demanded—£300—and the address to which it was to be sent: this time it was to Commander Blackleigh, Harrington Hotel, 76 Clonmel Gardens, Kensington.

Mrs. Samuelson went on:

"When Nanki Poo was safely back again, I went to the place myself, Mr. Poirot. After all, three hundred pounds is three hundred pounds."

"Certainly it is."

"The very first thing I saw was my letter enclosing the money in a kind of rack in the hall. Whilst I was waiting for the proprietress I slipped it into my bag. Unfortunately—"

Poirot said: "Unfortunately, when you opened it it contained only blank sheets of paper."

"How did you know?" Mrs. Samuelson turned on him with awe.

Poirot shrugged his shoulders.

"Obviously, chère Madame, the thief would take care to recover the money before he returned the dog. He would then replace the notes with blank paper and return the letter to the rack in case its absence should be noticed."

"No such person as Commander Blackleigh had ever stayed there."

Poirot smiled.

"And of course, my husband was extremely annoyed about the whole thing. In fact, he was livid—absolutely livid!"

Poirot murmured cautiously:

"You did not—er—consult him before dispatching the money?"

"Certainly not," said Mrs. Samuelson with decision.

Poirot looked a question. The lady explained.

"I wouldn't have risked it for a moment. Men are so extraordinary when it's a question of money. Jacob would have insisted on going to the police. I couldn't risk that. My poor darling Nanki Poo. Anything might have happened to him! Of course, I had to tell my husband afterwards, because I had to explain why I was overdrawn at the Bank."

Poirot murmured:

"Quite so—quite so."

"And I have really never seen him so angry. Men," said Mrs. Samuelson, rearranging her handsome diamond bracelet and turning her rings on her fingers, "think of nothing but money."

V

Hercule Poirot went up in the lift to Sir Joseph Hoggin's office. He sent in his card and was told that Sir Joseph was engaged at the moment but would see him presently. A haughty blonde sailed out of Sir Joseph's room at last with her hands full of papers. She gave the quaint little man a disdainful glance in passing.

Sir Joseph was seated behind his immense mahogany desk. There was a trace of lipstick on his chin.

"Well, Mr. Poirot? Sit down. Got any news for me?"

Hercule Poirot said:

"The whole affair is of a pleasing simplicity. In each case the money was sent to one of those boarding houses or private hotels where there is no porter or hall attendant and where a large number of guests are always coming and going, including a fairly large preponderance of ex-Service men. Nothing would be easier than for any one to walk in, abstract a letter from the rack, either take it away, or else remove the money and replace it with blank paper. Therefore, in every case, the trail ends abruptly in a blank wall."

"You mean you've no idea who the fellow is?"

"I have certain ideas, yes. It will take a few days to follow them up."

Sir Joseph looked at him curiously.

"Good work. Then, when you have got anything to report—"

"I will report to you at your house."

Sir Joseph said:

"If you get to the bottom of this business, it will be a pretty good piece of work."

Hercule Poirot said:

"There is no question of failure. Hercule Poirot does not fail."

Sir Joseph Hoggin looked at the little man and grinned.

"Sure of yourself, aren't you?" he demanded.

"Entirely with reason."

"Oh well." Sir Joseph Hoggin leaned back in his chair. "Pride goes before a fall, you know."

VI

Hercule Poirot, sitting in front of his electric radiator (and feeling a quiet satisfaction in its neat geometrical pattern) was giving instructions to his valet and general factotum.

"You understand, George?"

"Perfectly, sir."

"More probably a flat or maisonette. And it will definitely be within certain limits. South of the Park, east of Kensington Church, west of Knightsbridge Barracks and north of Fulham Road."

"I understand perfectly, sir."

Poirot murmured.

"A curious little case. There is evidence here of a very definite talent for organization. And there is, of course, the surprising invisibility of the star performer—the Nemean Lion himself, if I may so style him. Yes, an interesting little case. I could wish that I felt more attracted to my client—but he bears an unfortunate resemblance to a soap manufacturer of Liège who poisoned his wife in order to marry a blonde secretary. One of my early successes."

George shook his head. He said gravely:

"These blondes, sir, they're responsible for a lot of trouble."

VII

It was three days later when the invaluable George said:

"This is the address, sir."

Hercule Poirot took the piece of paper handed to him.

"Excellent, my good George. And what day of the week?"

"Thursdays, sir."

"Thursdays. And today, most fortunately, is a Thursday. So there need be no delay."

Twenty minutes later Hercule Poirot was climbing the stairs of an obscure block of flats tucked away in a little street leading off a more fashionable one. No. 10 Rosholm Mansions was on the third and top floor and there was no lift. Poirot toiled upwards round and round the narrow corkscrew staircase.

He paused to regain his breath on the top landing and from behind the door of No. 10 a new sound broke the silence—the sharp bark of a dog.

Hercule Poirot nodded his head with a slight smile. He pressed the bell of No. 10.

The barking redoubled—footsteps came to the door, it was opened. . . .

Miss Amy Carnaby fell back, her hand went to her ample breast.

"You permit that I enter?" said Hercule Poirot, and entered without waiting for the reply.

There was a sitting room door open on the right and he walked in. Behind him Miss Carnaby followed as though in a dream.

The room was very small and much overcrowded. Amongst the furniture a human being could be discovered, an elderly woman lying on a sofa drawn up to the gas fire. As Poirot came in, a Pekinese dog jumped off the sofa and came forward uttering a few sharp suspicious barks.

"Aha," said Poirot. "The chief actor! I salute you, my little friend."

He bent forward, extending his hand. The dog sniffed at it, his intelligent eyes fixed on the man's face.

Miss Carnaby muttered faintly:

"So you know?"

Hercule Poirot nodded.

"Yes, I know." He looked at the woman on the sofa. "Your sister, I think?"

Miss Carnaby said mechanically: "Yes, Emily, this—this is Mr. Poirot."

Emily Carnaby gave a gasp. She said: "Oh!"

Amy Carnaby said:

"Augustus. . . ."

The Pekinese looked towards her—his tail moved—then he resumed his scrutiny of Poirot's hand. Again his tail moved faintly.

Gently, Poirot picked the little dog up and sat down with Augustus on his knee. He said:

"So I have captured the Nemean Lion. My task is completed."

Amy Carnaby said in a hard dry voice:

"Do you really know everything?"

Poirot nodded.

"I think so. You organized this business—with Augustus to help you. You took your employer's dog out for his usual walk, brought him here and went on to the Park with Augustus. The Park Keeper saw you with a Pekinese as usual. The nurse girl, if we had ever found her, would also have agreed that you had a Pekinese with you when you spoke to her. Then, while you were talking, you cut the lead and Augustus, trained by you, slipped off at once and made a beeline back home. A few minutes later you gave the alarm that the dog had been stolen."

There was a pause. Then Miss Carnaby drew herself up with a certain pathetic dignity. She said:

"Yes. It is all quite true. I—I have nothing to say."

The invalid woman on the sofa began to cry softly.

Poirot said:

"Nothing at all, Mademoiselle?"

Miss Carnaby said:

"Nothing. I have been a thief—and now I am found out."

Poirot murmured:

"You have nothing to say—in your own defence?"

A spot of red showed suddenly in Amy Carnaby's white cheeks. She said:

"I—I don't regret what I did. I think that you are a kind man, Mr. Poirot, and that possibly you might understand. You see, I've been so terribly afraid."

                    The Plymouth Express Affair & Other Stories

"Afraid?"

"Yes, it's difficult for a gentleman to understand, I expect. But you see, I'm not a clever woman at all, and I've no training and I'm getting older—and I'm so terrified for the future. I've not been able to save anything—how could I with Emily to be cared for?—and as I get older and more incompetent there won't be any one who wants me. They'll want somebody young and brisk. I've—I've known so many people like I am—nobody wants you and you live in one room and you can't have a fire or any warmth and not very much to eat, and at last you can't even pay the rent of your room . . . There are Institutions, of course, but it's not very easy to get into them unless you have influential friends, and I haven't. There are a good many others situated like I am—poor companions—untrained useless women with nothing to look forward to but a deadly fear. . . ."

Her voice shook. She said:

"And so—some of us—got together and—and I thought of this. It was really having Augustus that put it into my mind. You see, to most people, one Pekinese is very much like another. (Just as we think the Chinese are.) Really, of course, it's ridiculous. No one who knew could mistake Augustus for Nanki Poo or Shan Tung or any of the other Pekes. He's far more intelligent for one thing, and he's much handsomer, but, as I say, to most people a Peke is just a Peke. Augustus put it into my head—that, combined with the fact that so many rich women have Pekinese dogs."

Poirot said with a faint smile:

"It must have been a profitable—racket! How many are there in the—the gang? Or perhaps I had better ask how often operations have been successfully carried out?"

Miss Carnaby said simply:

"Shan Tung was the sixteenth."

Hercule Poirot raised his eyebrows.

"I congratulate you. Your organization must have been indeed excellent."

Emily Carnaby said:

"Amy was always good at organization. Our father—he was the Vicar of Kellington in Essex—always said that Amy had quite a genius for planning. She always made all the arrangements for the Socials and the Bazaars and all that."

Poirot said with a little bow:

"I agree. As a criminal, Mademoiselle, you are quite in the first rank."

Amy Carnaby cried:

"A criminal. Oh dear, I suppose I am. But—but it never felt like that."

"How did it feel?"

"Of course, you are quite right. It was breaking the law. But you see—how can I explain it? Nearly all these women who employ us are so very rude and unpleasant. Lady Hoggin, for instance, doesn't mind what she says to me. She said her tonic tasted unpleasant the other day and practically accused me of tampering with it. All that sort of thing." Miss Carnaby flushed. "It's really very unpleasant. And not being able to say anything or answer back makes it rankle more, if you know what I mean."

"I know what you mean," said Hercule Poirot.

"And then seeing money frittered away so wastefully—that is upsetting. And Sir Joseph, occasionally he used to describe a coup he had made in the City—sometimes something that seemed to me (of course, I know I've only got a woman's brain and don't understand finance) downright dishonest. Well, you know, M. Poirot, it all—it all unsettled me, and I felt that to take a little money away from these people who really wouldn't miss it and hadn't been too scrupulous in acquiring it—well, really it hardly seemed wrong at all."

Poirot murmured:

"A modern Robin Hood! Tell me, Miss Carnaby, did you ever have to carry out the threats you used in your letters?"

  The Plymouth Express Affair & Other Stories

"Threats?"

"Were you ever compelled to mutilate the animals in the way you specified?"

Miss Carnaby regarded him in horror.

"Of course, I would never have dreamed of doing such a thing! That was just—just an artistic touch."

"Very artistic. It worked."

"Well, of course I knew it would. I know how I should have felt about Augustus, and of course I had to make sure these women never told their husbands until afterwards. The plan worked beautifully every time. In nine cases out of ten the companion was given the letter with the money to post. We usually steamed it open, took out the notes, and replaced them with paper. Once or twice the woman posted it herself. Then, of course, the companion had to go to the hotel and take the letter out of the rack. But that was quite easy, too."

"And the nursemaid touch? Was it always a nursemaid?"

"Well, you see, M. Poirot, old maids are known to be foolishly sentimental about babies. So it seemed quite natural that they should be absorbed over a baby and not notice anything."

Hercule Poirot sighed. He said:

"Your psychology is excellent, your organization is first class, and you are also a very fine actress. Your performance the other day when I interviewed Lady Hoggin was irreproachable. Never think of yourself disparagingly, Miss Carnaby. You may be what is termed an untrained woman but there is nothing wrong with your brains or with your courage."

Miss Carnaby said with a faint smile:

"And yet I have been found out, M. Poirot."

"Only by me. That was inevitable! When I had interviewed Mrs. Samuelson I realized that the kidnapping of Shan Tung was one of a series. I had already learned that you had once been left a Pekinese dog and had an invalid sister. I had only to ask my invaluable servant to look for a small flat within a certain radius occupied by an invalid lady who had a Pekinese dog and a sister who visited her once a week on her day out. It was simple."

Amy Carnaby drew herself up. She said:

"You have been very kind. It emboldens me to ask you a favour. I cannot, I know, escape the penalty for what I have done. I shall be sent to prison, I suppose. But if you could, M. Poirot, avert some of the publicity. So distressing for Emily—and for those few who knew us in the old days. I could not, I suppose, go to prison under a false name? Or is that a very wrong thing to ask?"

Hercule Poirot said:

"I think I can do more than that. But first of all I must make one thing quite clear. This ramp has got to stop. There must be no more disappearing dogs. All that is finished!"

"Yes! Oh yes!"

"And the money you extracted from Lady Hoggin must be returned."

Amy Carnaby crossed the room, opened the drawer of a bureau and returned with a packet of notes which she handed to Poirot.

"I was going to pay it into the pool today."

Poirot took the notes and counted them. He got up.

"I think it possible, Miss Carnaby, that I may be able to persuade Sir Joseph not to prosecute."

"Oh, M. Poirot!"

Amy Carnaby clasped her hands. Emily gave a cry of joy. Augustus barked and wagged his tail.

"As for you, mon ami," said Poirot addressing him. "There is one thing that I wish you would give me. It is your mantle of invisibility that I need. In all these cases nobody for a moment suspected that there was a second dog involved. Augustus possessed the lion's skin of invisibility."

"Of course, M. Poirot, according to the legend, Pekinese were lions once. And they still have the hearts of lions!"

"Augustus is, I suppose, the dog that was left to you by Lady Hartingfield and who is reported to have died? Were you never afraid of him coming home alone through the traffic?"

"Oh no, M. Poirot, Augustus is very clever about traffic. I have trained him most carefully. He has even grasped the principle of One Way Streets."

"In that case," said Hercule Poirot, "he is superior to most human beings!"

VIII

Sir Joseph received Hercule Poirot in his study. He said:

"Well, Mr. Poirot? Made your boast good?"

"Let me first ask you a question," said Poirot as he seated himself. "I know who the criminal is and I think it possible that I can produce sufficient evidence to convict this person. But in that case I doubt if you will ever recover your money."

"Not get back my money?"

Sir Joseph turned purple.

Hercule Poirot went on:

"But I am not a policeman. I am acting in this case solely in your interests. I could, I think, recover your money intact, if no proceedings were taken."

"Eh?" said Sir Joseph. "That needs a bit of thinking about."

"It is entirely for you to decide. Strictly speaking, I suppose you ought to prosecute in the public interest. Most people would say so."

"I dare say they would," said Sir Joseph sharply. "It wouldn't be their money that had gone west. If there's one thing I hate it's to be swindled. Nobody's ever swindled me and got away with it."

"Well then, what do you decide?"

Sir Joseph hit the table with his fist.

"I'll have the brass! Nobody's going to say they got away with two hundred pounds of my money."

Hercule Poirot rose, crossed to the writing table, wrote out a cheque for two hundred pounds and handed it to the other man.

Sir Joseph said in a weak voice:

"Well, I'm damned! Who the devil is this fellow?"

Poirot shook his head.

"If you accept the money, there must be no questions asked."

Sir Joseph folded up the cheque and put it in his pocket.

"That's a pity. But the money's the thing. And what do I owe you, Mr. Poirot?"

"My fees will not be high. This was, as I said, a very unimportant matter." He paused—and added, "Nowadays nearly all my cases are murder cases. . . ."

Sir Joseph started slightly.

"Must be interesting?" he said.

"Sometimes. Curiously enough, you recall to me one of my earlier cases in Belgium, many years ago—the chief protagonist was very like you in appearance. He was a wealthy soap manufacturer. He poisoned his wife in order to be free to marry his secretary . . . Yes—the resemblance is very remarkable. . . ."

A faint sound came from Sir Joseph's lips—they had gone a queer blue colour. All the ruddy hue had faded from his cheeks. His eyes, starting out of his head, stared at Poirot. He slipped down a little in his chair.

Then, with a shaking hand, he fumbled in his pocket. He drew out the cheque and tore it into pieces.

"That's washed out—see? Consider it as your fee."

"Oh but, Sir Joseph, my fee would not have been as large as that."

"That's all right. You keep it."

"I shall send it to a deserving charity."

"Send it anywhere you damn well like."

Poirot leaned forward. He said:

"I think I need hardly point out, Sir Joseph, that in your position, you would do well to be exceedingly careful."

Sir Joseph said, his voice almost inaudible:

"You needn't worry. I shall be careful all right."

Hercule Poirot left the house. As he went down the steps he said to himself:

"So—I was right."

IX

Lady Hoggin said to her husband:

"Funny, this tonic tastes quite different. It hasn't got that bitter taste any more. I wonder why?"

Sir Joseph growled:

"Chemist. Careless fellows. Make things up differently different times."

Lady Hoggin said doubtfully:

"I suppose that must be it."

"Of course it is. What else could it be?"

"Has the man found out anything about Shan Tung?"

"Yes. He got me my money back all right."

"Who was it?"

"He didn't say. Very close fellow, Hercule Poirot. But you needn't worry."

"He's a funny little man, isn't he?"

Sir Joseph gave a slight shiver and threw a sideways glance upwards as though he felt the invisible presence of Hercule Poirot behind his right shoulder. He had an idea that he would always feel it there.

He said:

"He's a damned clever little devil!"

And he thought to himself:

"Greta can go hang! I'm not going to risk my neck for any damned platinum blonde!"

X

"Oh!"

Amy Carnaby gazed down incredulously at the cheque for two hundred pounds. She cried:

"Emily! Emily! Listen to this.

'Dear Miss Carnaby,

Allow me to enclose a contribution to your very deserving Fund before it is finally wound up.

Yours very truly,

Hercule Poirot.' "

"Amy," said Emily Carnaby, "you've been incredibly lucky. Think where you might be now."

"Wormwood Scrubbs—or is it Holloway?" murmured Amy Carnaby. "But that's all over now—isn't it, Augustus? No more walks to the Park with mother or mother's friends and a little pair of scissors."

A far away wistfulness came into her eyes. She sighed.

"Dear Augustus! It seems a pity. He's so clever . . . One can teach him anything. . . ."

The Labors of Hercules

Hercule Poirot's flat was essentially modern in its furnishings. It gleamed with chromium. Its easy chairs, though comfortably padded, were square and uncompromising in outline.

On one of these chairs sat Hercule Poirot, neatly—in the middle of the chair. Opposite him, in another chair, sat Dr. Burton, Fellow of All Souls, sipping appreciatively at a glass of Poirot's Château Mouton Rothschild. There was no neatness about Dr. Burton. He was plump, untidy, and beneath his thatch of white hair beamed a rubicund and benign countenance. He had a deep wheezy chuckle and the habit of covering himself and everything round him with tobacco ash. In vain did Poirot surround him with ashtrays.

Dr. Burton was asking a question.

"Tell me," he said. "Why Hercule?"

"You mean, my Christian name?"

"Hardly a Christian name," the other demurred. "Definitely pagan. But why? That's what I want to know. Father's fancy? Mother's whim? Family reasons? If I remember rightly—though my memory isn't what it was—you had a brother called Achille, did you not?"

Poirot's mind raced back over the details of Achille Poirot's career. Had all that really happened?

"Only for a short space of time," he replied.

Dr. Burton passed tactfully from the subject of Achille Poirot.

"People should be more careful how they name their children," he ruminated. "I've got godchildren. I know. Blanche, one of 'em is called—dark as a gypsy! Then there's Deirdre, Deirdre of the Sorrows—she's turned out merry as a grig. As for young Patience, she might as well have been named Impatience and be done with it! And Diana—well, Diana—" the old classical scholar shuddered. "Weighs twelve stone now—and she's only fifteen! They say it's puppy fat—but it doesn't look that way to me. Diana! They wanted to call her Helen, but I did put my foot down there. Knowing what her father and mother looked like! And her grandmother for that matter! I tried hard for Martha or Dorcas or something sensible—but it was no good—waste of breath. Rum people, parents. . . ."

He began to wheeze gently—his small fat face crinkled up.

Poirot looked at him inquiringly.

"Thinking of an imaginary conversation. Your mother and the late Mrs. Holmes, sitting sewing little garments or knitting: 'Achille, Hercule, Sherlock, Mycroft. . . .' "

Poirot failed to share his friend's amusement.

"What I understand you to mean is, that in physical appearance I do not resemble a Hercules?"

Dr. Burton's eyes swept over Hercule Poirot, over his small neat person attired in striped trousers, correct black jacket and natty bow tie, swept up from his patent leather shoes to his egg-shaped head and the immense moustache that adorned his upper lip.

"Frankly, Poirot," said Dr. Burton, "you don't! I gather," he added, "that you've never had much time to study the Classics?"

"That is so."

"Pity. Pity. You've missed a lot. Everyone should be made to study the Classics if I had my way."

Poirot shrugged his shoulders.

"Eh bien, I have got on very well without them."

"Got on! Got on! It's not a question of getting on. That's the wrong view altogether. The Classics aren't a ladder leading to quick success like a modern correspondence course! It's not a man's working hours that are important—it's his leisure hours. That's the mistake we all make. Take yourself now, you're getting on, you'll be wanting to get out of things, to take things easy—what are you going to do then with your leisure hours?"

Poirot was ready with his reply.

"I am going to attend—seriously—to the cultivation of vegetable marrows."

Dr. Burton was taken aback.

"Vegetable marrows? What d'yer mean? Those great swollen green things that taste of water?"

"Ah," Poirot spoke enthusiastically. "But that is the whole point of it. They need not taste of water."

"Oh! I know—sprinkle 'em with cheese, or minced onion or white sauce."

"No, no—you are in error. It is my idea that the actual flavour of the marrow itself can be improved. It can be given," he screwed up his eyes, "a bouquet—"

"Good God, man, it's not a claret." The word bouquet reminded Dr. Burton of the glass at his elbow. He sipped and savoured. "Very good wine, this. Very sound. Yes." His head nodded in approbation. "But this vegetable marrow business—you're not serious? You don't mean"—he spoke in lively horror—"that you're actually going to stoop"—his hands descended in sympathetic horror on his own plump stomach—"stoop, and fork dung on the things, and feed 'em with strands of wool dipped in water and all the rest of it?"

"You seem," Poirot said, "to be well acquainted with the culture of the marrow?"

"Seen gardeners doing it when I've been staying in the country. But seriously, Poirot, what a hobby! Compare that to"—his voice sank to an appreciative purr—"an easy chair in front of a wood fire in a long, low room lined with books—must be a long room—not a square one. Books all round one. A glass of port—and a book open in your hand. Time rolls back as you read:" he quoted sonorously:

He translated:

" 'By skill again, the pilot on the wine-dark sea straightens

The swift ship buffeted by the winds.'

Of course you can never really get the spirit of the original."

For the moment, in his enthusiasm, he had forgotten Poirot. And Poirot, watching him, felt suddenly a doubt—an uncomfortable twinge. Was there, here, something that he had missed? Some richness of the spirit? Sadness crept over him. Yes, he should have become acquainted with the Classics . . . Long ago . . . Now, alas, it was too late. . . .

Dr. Burton interrupted his melancholy.

"Do you mean that you really are thinking of retiring?"

"Yes."

The other chuckled.

"You won't!"

"But I assure you—"

"You won't be able to do it, man. You're too interested in your work."

"No—indeed—I make all the arrangements. A few more cases— specially selected ones—not, you understand, everything that presents itself—just problems that have a personal appeal."

Dr. Burton grinned.

"That's the way of it. Just a case or two, just one case more—and so on. The Prima Donna's farewell performance won't be in it with yours, Poirot!"

He chuckled and rose slowly to his feet, an amiable white-haired gnome.

"Yours aren't the Labors of Hercules," he said. "Yours are labors of love. You'll see if I'm not right. Bet you that in twelve months' time you'll still be here, and vegetable marrows will still be"—he shuddered—"merely marrows."

Taking leave of his host, Dr. Burton left the severe rectangular room.

He passes out of these pages not to return to them. We are concerned only with what he left behind him, which was an Idea.

For after his departure Hercule Poirot sat down again slowly like a man in a dream and murmured:

"The Labors of Hercules . . . Mais oui, c'est une idée, ça. . . ."

The following day saw Hercule Poirot perusing a large calf-bound volume and other slimmer works, with occasional harried glances at various typewritten slips of paper.

His secretary, Miss Lemon, had been detailed to collect information on the subject of Hercules and to place same before him.

Without interest (hers not the type to wonder why!) but with perfect efficiency, Miss Lemon had fulfilled her task.

Hercule Poirot was plunged head first into a bewildering sea of classical lore with particular reference to "Hercules, a celebrated hero who, after death, was ranked among the gods, and received divine honours."

So far, so good—but thereafter it was far from plain sailing. For two hours Poirot read diligently, making notes, frowning, consulting his slips of paper and his other books of reference. Finally he sank back in his chair and shook his head. His mood of the previous evening was dispelled. What people!

Take this Hercules—this hero! Hero, indeed! What was he but a large muscular creature of low intelligence and criminal tendencies! Poirot was reminded of one Adolfe Durand, a butcher, who had been tried at Lyon in 1895—a creature of oxlike strength who had killed several children. The defence had been epilepsy—from which he undoubtedly suffered—though whether grand mal or petit mal had been an argument of several days' discussion. This ancient Hercules probably suffered from grand mal. No, Poirot shook his head, if that was the Greeks' idea of a hero, then measured by modern standards it certainly would not do. The whole classical pattern shocked him. These gods and goddesses—they seemed to have as many different aliases as a modern criminal. Indeed they seemed to be definitely criminal types. Drink, debauchery, incest, rape, loot, homicide and chicanery—enough to keep a juge d'Instruction constantly busy. No decent family life. No order, no method. Even in their crimes, no order or method!

"Hercules indeed!" said Hercule Poirot, rising to his feet, disillusioned.

He looked round him with approval. A square room, with good square modern furniture—even a piece of good modern sculpture representing one cube placed on another cube and above it a geometrical arrangement of copper wire. And in the midst of this shining and orderly room, himself. He looked at himself in the glass. Here, then, was a modern Hercules—very distinct from that unpleasant sketch of a naked figure with bulging muscles, brandishing a club. Instead, a small compact figure attired in correct urban wear with a moustache—such a moustache as Hercules never dreamed of cultivating—a moustache magnificent yet sophisticated.

Yet there was between this Hercule Poirot and the Hercules of Classical lore one point of resemblance. Both of them, undoubtedly, had been instrumental in ridding the world of certain pests . . . Each of them could be described as a benefactor to the Society he lived in. . . .

What had Dr. Burton said last night as he left: "Yours are not the Labors of Hercules. . . ."

Ah, but there he was wrong, the old fossil. There should be, once again, the Labors of Hercules—a modern Hercules. An ingenious and amusing conceit! In the period before his final retirement he would accept twelve cases, no more, no less. And those twelve cases should be selected with special reference to the twelve Labors of ancient Hercules. Yes, that would not only be amusing, it would be artistic, it would be spiritual.

Poirot picked up the Classical Dictionary and immersed himself once more in Classical lore. He did not intend to follow his prototype too closely. There should be no women, no shirt of Nessus . . . The Labors and the Labors only.

The first Labor, then, would be that of the Nemean Lion.

"The Nemean Lion," he repeated, trying it over on his tongue.

Naturally he did not expect a case to present itself actually involving a flesh and blood lion. It would be too much of a coincidence should he be approached by the Directors of the Zoological Gardens to solve a problem for them involving a real lion.

No, here symbolism must be involved. The first case must concern some celebrated public figure, it must be sensational and of the first importance! Some master criminal—or alternately someone who was a lion in the public eye. Some well-known writer, or politician, or painter—or even Royalty?

He liked the idea of Royalty. . . .

He would not be in a hurry. He would wait—wait for that case of high importance that should be the first of his self-imposed Labors.

The Stymphalean Birds

Harold Waring noticed them first walking up the path from the lake. He was sitting outside the hotel on the terrace. The day was fine, the lake was blue, and the sun shone. Harold was smoking a pipe and feeling that the world was a pretty good place.

His political career was shaping well. An undersecretaryship at the age of thirty was something to be justly proud of. It had been reported that the Prime Minister had said to someone that "young Waring would go far." Harold was, not unnaturally, elated. Life presented itself to him in rosy colours. He was young, sufficiently good-looking, in first-class condition, and quite unencumbered with romantic ties.

He had decided to take a holiday in Herzoslovakia so as to get right off the beaten track and have a real rest from everyone and everything. The hotel at Lake Stempka, though small, was comfortable and not overcrowded. The few people there were mostly foreigners. So far the only other English people were an elderly woman, Mrs. Rice, and her married daughter, Mrs. Clayton. Harold liked them both. Elsie Clayton was pretty in a rather old-fashioned style. She made up very little, if at all, and was gentle and rather shy. Mrs. Rice was what is called a woman of character. She was tall, with a deep voice and a masterful manner, but she had a sense of humour and was good company. Her life was clearly bound up in that of her daughter.

Harold had spent some pleasant hours in the company of mother and daughter, but they did not attempt to monopolize him and relations remained friendly and unexacting between them.

The other people in the hotel had not aroused Harold's notice. Usually they were hikers, or members of a motor-coach tour. They stayed a night or two and then went on. He had hardly noticed any one else—until this afternoon.

They came up the path from the lake very slowly and it just happened that at the moment when Harold's attention was attracted to them, a cloud came over the sun. He shivered a little.

Then he stared. Surely there was something odd about these two women? They had long, curved noses, like birds, and their faces, which were curiously alike, were quite immobile. Over their shoulders they wore loose cloaks that flapped in the wind like the wings of two big birds.

Harold thought to himself.

"They are like birds—" he added almost without volition, "birds of ill omen."

The women came straight up on the terrace and passed close by him. They were not young—perhaps nearer fifty than forty, and the resemblance between them was so close that they were obviously sisters. Their expression was forbidding. As they passed Harold the eyes of both of them rested on him for a minute. It was a curious, appraising glance—almost inhuman.

Harold's impression of evil grew stronger. He noticed the hand of one of the two sisters, a long clawlike hand . . . Although the sun had come out, he shivered once again. He thought:

"Horrible creatures. Like birds of prey. . . ."

He was distracted from these imaginings by the emergence of Mrs. Rice from the hotel. He jumped up and drew forward a chair. With a word of thanks she sat down and, as usual, began to knit vigorously.

Harold asked:

"Did you see those two women who just went into the hotel?"

"With cloaks on? Yes, I passed them."

"Extraordinary creatures, didn't you think?"

"Well—yes, perhaps they are rather odd. They only arrived yesterday, I think. Very alike—they must be twins."

Harold said:

"I may be fanciful, but I distinctly felt there was something evil about them."

"How curious. I must look at them more closely and see if I agree with you."

She added: "We'll find out from the concierge who they are. Not English, I imagine?"

"Oh no."

Mrs. Rice glanced at her watch. She said:

"Teatime. I wonder if you'd mind going in and ringing the bell, Mr. Waring?"

"Certainly, Mrs. Rice."

He did so and then as he returned to his seat he asked:

"Where's your daughter this afternoon?"

"Elsie? We went for a walk together. Part of the way round the lake and then back through the pinewoods. It really was lovely."

A waiter came out and received orders for tea. Mrs. Rice went on, her needles flying vigorously:

"Elsie had a letter from her husband. She mayn't come down to tea."

"Her husband?" Harold was surprised. "Do you know, I always thought she was a widow."

Mrs. Rice shot him a sharp glance. She said drily:

"Oh no, Elsie isn't a widow." She added with emphasis: "Unfortunately!"

Harold was startled.

Mrs. Rice, nodding her head grimly, said:

"Drink is responsible for a lot of unhappiness, Mr. Waring."

"Does he drink?"

"Yes. And a good many other things as well. He's insanely jealous and has a singularly violent temper." She sighed. "It's a difficult world, Mr. Waring. I'm devoted to Elsie, she's my only child—and to see her unhappy isn't an easy thing to bear."

Harold said with real emotion:

"She's such a gentle creature."

"A little too gentle, perhaps."

"You mean—"

Mrs. Rice said slowly:

"A happy creature is more arrogant. Elsie's gentleness comes, I think, from a sense of defeat. Life has been too much for her."

Harold said with some slight hesitation:

"How—did she come to marry this husband of hers?"

Mrs. Rice answered:

"Philip Clayton was a very attractive person. He had (still has) great charm, he had a certain amount of money—and there was no one to advise us of his real character. I had been a widow for many years. Two women, living alone, are not the best judges of a man's character."

Harold said thoughtfully:

"No, that's true."

He felt a wave of indignation and pity sweep over him. Elsie Clayton could not be more than twenty-five at the most. He recalled the clear friendliness of her blue eyes, the soft droop of her mouth. He realized, suddenly, that his interest in her went a little beyond friendship.

And she was tied to a brute. . . .

II

That evening, Harold joined mother and daughter after dinner. Elsie Clayton was wearing a soft dull pink dress. Her eyelids, he noticed, were red. She had been crying.

Mrs. Rice said briskly:

"I've found out who your two harpies are, Mr. Waring. Polish ladies—of very good family, so the concierge says."

Harold looked across the room to where the Polish ladies were sitting. Elsie said with interest:

"Those two women over there? With the henna-dyed hair? They look rather horrible somehow—I don't know why."

Harold said triumphantly:

"That's just what I thought."

Mrs. Rice said with a laugh:

"I think you are both being absurd. You can't possibly tell what people are like just by looking at them."

Elsie laughed.

She said:

"I suppose one can't. All the same I think they're vultures!"

"Picking out dead men's eyes!" said Harold.

"Oh, don't," cried Elsie.

Harold said quickly:

"Sorry."

Mrs. Rice said with a smile:

"Anyway they're not likely to cross our path."

Elsie said:

"We haven't got any guilty secrets!"

"Perhaps Mr. Waring has," said Mrs. Rice with a twinkle.

Harold laughed, throwing his head back.

He said:

"Not a secret in the world. My life's an open book."

And it flashed across his mind:

"What fools people are who leave the straight path. A clear conscience—that's all one needs in life. With that you can face the world and tell everyone who interferes with you to go to the devil!"

He felt suddenly very much alive—very strong—very much master of his fate!

III

Harold Waring, like many other Englishmen, was a bad linguist. His French was halting and decidedly British in intonation. Of German and Italian he knew nothing.

Up to now, these linguistic disabilities had not worried him. In most hotels on the Continent, he had always found, everyone spoke English, so why worry?

But in this out-of-the-way spot, where the native language was a form of Slovak and even the concierge only spoke German it was sometimes galling to Harold when one of his two women friends acted as interpreter for him. Mrs. Rice, who was fond of languages, could even speak a little Slovak.

Harold determined that he would set about learning German. He decided to buy some textbooks and spend a couple of hours each morning in mastering the language.

The morning was fine and after writing some letters, Harold looked at his watch and saw that there was still time for an hour's stroll before lunch. He went down towards the lake and then turned aside into the pine woods. He had walked there for perhaps five minutes when he heard an unmistakable sound. Somewhere not far away a woman was sobbing her heart out.

Harold paused a minute, then he went in the direction of the sound. The woman was Elsie Clayton and she was sitting on a fallen tree with her face buried in her hands and her shoulders quivering with the violence of her grief.

Harold hesitated a minute, then he came up to her. He said gently:

"Mrs. Clayton—Elsie?"

She started violently and looked up at him. Harold sat down beside her.

He said with real sympathy:

"Is there anything I can do? Anything at all?"

She shook her head.

"No—no—you're very kind. But there's nothing that anyone can do for me."

Harold said rather diffidently:

"Is it to do with—your husband?"

She nodded. Then she wiped her eyes and took out her powder compact, struggling to regain command of herself. She said in a quavering voice:

"I didn't want Mother to worry. She's so upset when she sees me unhappy. So I came out here to have a good cry. It's silly, I know. Crying doesn't help. But—sometimes—one just feels that life is quite unbearable."

Harold said:

"I'm terribly sorry."

She threw him a grateful glance. Then she said hurriedly:

 The Plymouth Express Affair & Other Stories

"It's my own fault, of course. I married Philip of my own free will. It—it's turned out badly, I've only myself to blame."

Harold said:

"It's very plucky of you to put it like that."

Elsie shook her head.

"No, I'm not plucky. I'm not brave at all. I'm an awful coward. That's partly the trouble with Philip. I'm terrified of him—absolutely terrified—when he gets in one of his rages."

Harold said with feeling:

"You ought to leave him!"

"I daren't. He—he wouldn't let me."

"Nonsense! What about a divorce?"

She shook her head slowly.

"I've no grounds." She straightened her shoulders. "No, I've got to carry on. I spend a fair amount of time with Mother, you know. Philip doesn't mind that. Especially when we go somewhere off the beaten track like this." She added, the colour rising in her cheeks, "You see, part of the trouble is that he's insanely jealous. If—if I so much as speak to another man he makes the most frightful scenes."

Harold's indignation rose. He had heard many women complain of the jealousy of a husband, and whilst professing sympathy, had been secretly of the opinion that the husband was amply justified. But Elsie Clayton was not one of those women. She had never thrown him so much as a flirtatious glance.

Elsie drew away from him with a slight shiver. She glanced up at the sky.

"The sun's gone in. It's quite cold. We'd better get back to the hotel. It must be nearly lunchtime."

They got up and turned in the direction of the hotel. They had walked for perhaps a minute when they overtook a figure going in the same direction. They recognized her by the flapping cloak she wore. It was one of the Polish sisters.

They passed her, Harold bowing slightly. She made no response but her eyes rested on them both for a minute and there was a certain appraising quality in the glance which made Harold feel suddenly hot. He wondered if the woman had seen him sitting by Elsie on the tree trunk. If so, she probably thought. . . .

Well, she looked as though she thought . . . A wave of indignation overwhelmed him! What foul minds some women had!

Odd that the sun had gone in and that they should both have shivered—perhaps just at the moment that that woman was watching them. . . .

Somehow, Harold felt a little uneasy.

IV

That evening, Harold went to his room a little after ten. The English maid had arrived and he had received a number of letters, some of which needed immediate answers.

He got into his pyjamas and a dressing gown and sat down at the desk to deal with his correspondence. He had written three letters and was just starting on the fourth when the door was suddenly flung open and Elsie Clayton staggered into the room.

Harold jumped up, startled. Elsie had pushed the door to behind her and was standing clutching at the chest of drawers. Her breath was coming in great gasps, her face was the colour of chalk. She looked frightened to death.

She gasped out: "It's my husband! He arrived unexpectedly. I—I think he'll kill me. He's mad—quite mad. I came to you. Don't—don't let him find me."

She took a step or two forward, swaying so much that she almost fell. Harold put out an arm to support her.

As he did so, the door was flung open and a man stood in the doorway. He was of medium height with thick eyebrows and a sleek, dark head. In his hand he carried a heavy car spanner. His voice rose high and shook with rage. He almost screamed the words.

"So that Polish woman was right! You are carrying on with this fellow!"

Elsie cried:

"No, no, Philip. It's not true. You're wrong."

Harold thrust the girl swiftly behind him, as Philip Clayton advanced on them both. The latter cried:

"Wrong, am I? When I find you here in his room? You she-devil, I'll kill you for this."

With a swift, sideways movement he dodged Harold's arm. Elsie, with a cry, ran round the other side of Harold, who swung round to fend the other off.

But Philip Clayton had only one idea, to get at his wife. He swerved round again. Elsie, terrified, rushed out of the room. Philip Clayton dashed after her, and Harold, with not a moment's hesitation, followed him.

Elsie had darted back into her own bedroom at the end of the corridor. Harold could hear the sound of the key turning in the lock, but it did not turn in time. Before the lock could catch Philip Clayton wrenched the door open. He disappeared into the room and Harold heard Elsie's frightened cry. In another minute Harold burst in after them.

Elsie was standing at bay against the curtains of the window. As Harold entered Philip Clayton rushed at her brandishing the spanner. She gave a terrified cry, then snatching up a heavy paperweight from the desk beside her, she flung it at him.

Clayton went down like a log. Elsie screamed. Harold stopped petrified in the doorway. The girl fell on her knees beside her husband. He lay quite still where he had fallen.

Outside in the passage, there was the sound of the bolt of one of the doors being drawn back. Elsie jumped up and ran to Harold.

"Please—please—" Her voice was low and breathless. "Go back to your room. They'll come—they'll find you here."

Harold nodded. He took in the situation like lightning. For the moment, Philip Clayton was hors de combat. But Elsie's scream might have been heard. If he were found in her room it could only cause embarrassment and misunderstanding. Both for her sake and his own there must be no scandal.

As noiselessly as possible, he sprinted down the passage and back into his room. Just as he reached it, he heard the sound of an opening door.

He sat in his room for nearly half an hour, waiting. He dared not go out. Sooner or later, he felt sure, Elsie would come.

There was a light tap on his door. Harold jumped up to open it.

It was not Elsie who came in but her mother and Harold was aghast at her appearance. She looked suddenly years older. Her grey hair was dishevelled and there were deep black circles under her eyes.

He sprang up and helped her to a chair. She sat down, her breath coming painfully. Harold said quickly:

"You look all in, Mrs. Rice. Can I get you something?"

She shook her head.

"No. Never mind me. I'm all right, really. It's only the shock. Mr. Waring, a terrible thing has happened."

Harold asked:

"Is Clayton seriously injured?"

She caught her breath.

"Worse than that. He's dead . . ."

V

The room spun round.

A feeling as of icy water trickling down his spine rendered Harold incapable of speech for a moment or two.

He repeated dully:

"Dead?"

Mrs. Rice nodded.

She said, and her voice had the flat level tones of complete exhaustion:

"The corner of that marble paperweight caught him right on the temple and he fell back with his head on the iron fender. I don't know which it was that killed him—but he is certainly dead. I have seen death often enough to know."

Disaster—that was the word that rang insistently in Harold's brain. Disaster, disaster, disaster. . . .

He said vehemently:

"It was an accident . . . I saw it happen."

Mrs. Rice said sharply:

"Of course it was an accident. I know that. But—but—is anyone else going to think so? I'm—frankly, I'm frightened, Harold! This isn't England."

Harold said slowly:

"I can confirm Elsie's story."

Mrs. Rice said:

"Yes, and she can confirm yours. That—that is just it!"

Harold's brain, naturally a keen and cautious one, saw her point. He reviewed the whole thing and appreciated the weakness of their position.

He and Elsie had spent a good deal of their time together. Then there was the fact that they had been seen together in the pinewoods by one of the Polish women under rather compromising circumstances. The Polish ladies apparently spoke no English, but they might nevertheless understand it a little. The woman might have known the meaning of words like "jealousy" and "husband" if she had chanced to overhear their conversation. Anyway it was clear that it was something she had said to Clayton that had aroused his jealousy. And now—his death. When Clayton had died, he, Harold, had been in Elsie Clayton's room. There was nothing to show that he had not deliberately assaulted Philip Clayton with the paperweight. Nothing to show that the jealous husband had not actually found them together. There was only his word and Elsie's. Would they be believed?

A cold fear gripped him.

He did not imagine—no, he really did not imagine—that either he or Elsie was in danger of being condemned to death for a murder they had not committed. Surely, in any case, it could be only a charge of manslaughter brought against them. (Did they have manslaughter in these foreign countries?) But even if they were acquitted of blame there would have to be an inquiry—it would be reported in all the papers. An English man and woman accused—jealous husband—rising politician. Yes, it would mean the end of his political career. It would never survive a scandal like that.

He said on an impulse:

"Can't we get rid of the body somehow? Plant it somewhere?"

Mrs. Rice's astonished and scornful look made him blush. She said incisively:

 The Plymouth Express Affair & Other Stories

"My dear Harold, this isn't a detective story! To attempt a thing like that would be quite crazy."

"I suppose it would." He groaned. "What can we do? My God, what can we do?"

Mrs. Rice shook her head despairingly. She was frowning, her mind working painfully.

Harold demanded:

"Isn't there anything we can do? Anything to avoid this frightful disaster?"

There, it was out—disaster! Terrible—unforeseen—utterly damning.

They stared at each other. Mrs. Rice said hoarsely:

"Elsie—my little girl. I'd do anything . . . It will kill her if she has to go through a thing like this." And she added: "You too, your career—everything."

Harold managed to say:

"Never mind me."

But he did not really mean it.

Mrs. Rice went on bitterly:

"And all so unfair—so utterly untrue! It's not as though there had ever been anything between you. I know that well enough."

Harold suggested, catching at a straw:

"You'll be able to say that at least—that it was all perfectly all right."

Mrs. Rice said bitterly:

"Yes, if they believe me. But you know what these people out here are like!"

Harold agreed gloomily. To the Continental mind, there would undoubtedly be a guilty connection between himself and Elsie, and all Mrs. Rice's denials would be taken as a mother lying herself black in the face for her daughter.

Harold said gloomily:

"Yes, we're not in England, worse luck."

"Ah!" Mrs. Rice lifted her head. "That's true . . . It's not England. I wonder now if something could be done—"

"Yes?" Harold looked at her eagerly.

Mrs. Rice said abruptly:

"How much money have you got?"

"Not much with me." He added, "I could wire for money, of course."

Mrs. Rice said grimly:

"We may need a good deal. But I think it's worth trying."

Harold felt a faint lifting of despair. He said:

"What is your idea?"

Mrs. Rice spoke decisively.

"We haven't a chance of concealing the death ourselves, but I do think there's just a chance of hushing it up officially!"

"You really think so?" Harold was hopeful but slightly incredulous.

"Yes, for one thing the manager of the hotel will be on our side. He'd much rather have the thing hushed up. It's my opinion that in these out of the way curious little Balkan countries you can bribe anyone and everyone—and the police are probably more corrupt than anyone else!"

Harold said slowly:

"Do you know, I believe you're right."

Mrs. Rice went on:

"Fortunately, I don't think anyone in the hotel heard anything."

"Who has the room next to Elsie's on the other side from yours?"

"The two Polish ladies. They didn't hear anything. They'd have come out into the passage if they had. Philip arrived late, nobody saw him but the night porter. Do you know, Harold, I believe it will be possible to hush the whole thing up—and get Philip's death certified as due to natural causes! It's just a question of bribing high enough—and finding the right man—probably the Chief of Police!"

Harold smiled faintly. He said:

"It's rather Comic Opera, isn't it? Well, after all, we can but try."

VI

Mrs. Rice was energy personified. First the manager was summoned. Harold remained in his room, keeping out of it. He and Mrs. Rice had agreed that the story told had better be that of a quarrel between husband and wife. Elsie's youth and prettiness would command more sympathy.

On the following morning various police officials arrived and were shown up to Mrs. Rice's bedroom. They left at midday. Harold had wired for money but otherwise had taken no part in the proceedings—indeed he would have been unable to do so since none of these official personages spoke English.

At twelve o'clock Mrs. Rice came to his room. She looked white and tired, but the relief on her face told its own story. She said simply:

"It's worked!"

"Thank heaven! You've been really marvellous! It seems incredible!"

Mrs. Rice said thoughtfully:

"By the ease with which it went, you might almost think it was quite normal. They practically held out their hands right away. It's—it's rather disgusting, really!"

Harold said dryly:

"This isn't the moment to quarrel with the corruption of the public services. How much?"

"The tariff's rather high."

She read out a list of figures.

"The Chief of Police.

The Commissaire.

The Agent.

The Doctor.

The Hotel Manager.

The Night Porter."

Harold's comment was merely:

"The night porter doesn't get much, does he? I suppose it's mostly a question of gold lace."

Mrs. Rice explained:

"The manager stipulated that the death should not have taken place in his hotel at all. The official story will be that Philip had a heart attack in the train. He went along the corridor for air—you know how they always leave those doors open—and he fell out on the line. It's wonderful what the police can do when they try!"

"Well," said Harold. "Thank God our police force isn't like that."

And in a British and superior mood he went down to lunch.

VII

After lunch Harold usually joined Mrs. Rice and her daughter for coffee. He decided to make no change in his usual behaviour.

This was the first time he had seen Elsie since the night before. She was very pale and was obviously still suffering from shock, but she made a gallant endeavour to behave as usual, uttering small commonplaces about the weather and the scenery.

They commented on a new guest who had just arrived, trying to guess his nationality. Harold thought a moustache like that must be French—Elsie said German—and Mrs. Rice thought he might be Spanish.

There was no one else but themselves on the terrace with the exception of the two Polish ladies who were sitting at the extreme end, both doing fancywork.

As always when he saw them, Harold felt a queer shiver of apprehension pass over him. Those still faces, those curved beaks of noses, those long clawlike hands. . . .

A page boy approached and told Mrs. Rice she was wanted. She rose and followed him. At the entrance to the hotel they saw her encounter a police official in full uniform.

Elsie caught her breath.

"You don't think—anything's gone wrong?"

Harold reassured her quickly.

"Oh, no, no, nothing of that kind."

But he himself knew a sudden pang of fear.

He said:

"Your mother's been wonderful!"

"I know. Mother is a great fighter. She'll never sit down under defeat." Elsie shivered. "But it is all horrible, isn't it?"

"Now, don't dwell on it. It's all over and done with."

Elsie said in a low voice:

"I can't forget that—that it was I who killed him."

Harold said urgently:

"Don't think of it that way. It was an accident. You know that really."

Her face grew a little happier. Harold added:

"And anyway it's past. The past is the past. Try never to think of it again."

Mrs. Rice came back. By the expression on her face they saw that all was well.

"It gave me quite a fright," she said almost gaily. "But it was only a formality about some papers. Everything's all right, my children. We're out of the shadow. I think we might order ourselves a liqueur on the strength of it."

The liqueur was ordered and came. They raised their glasses.

Mrs. Rice said: "To the Future!"

Harold smiled at Elsie and said:

"To your happiness!"

She smiled back at him and said as she lifted her glass:

"And to you—to your success! I'm sure you're going to be a very great man."

With the reaction from fear they felt gay, almost light-headed. The shadow had lifted! All was well. . . .

From the far end of the terrace the two birdlike women rose. They rolled up their work carefully. They came across the stone flags.

With little bows they sat down by Mrs. Rice. One of them began to speak. The other one let her eyes rest on Elsie and Harold. There was a little smile on her lips. It was not, Harold thought, a nice smile. . . .

He looked over at Mrs. Rice. She was listening to the Polish woman and though he couldn't understand a word, the expression on Mrs. Rice's face was clear enough. All the old anguish and despair came back. She listened and occasionally spoke a brief word.

Presently the two sisters rose, and with stiff little bows went into the hotel.

Harold leaned forward. He said hoarsely:

"What is it?"

Mrs. Rice answered him in the quiet hopeless tones of despair.

"Those women are going to blackmail us. They heard everything last night. And now we've tried to hush it up, it makes the whole thing a thousand times worse . . ."

VIII

Harold Waring was down by the lake. He had been walking feverishly for over an hour, trying by sheer physical energy to still the clamour of despair that had attacked him.

He came at last to the spot where he had first noticed the two grim women who held his life and Elsie's in their evil talons. He said aloud:

"Curse them! Damn them for a pair of devilish bloodsucking harpies!"

A slight cough made him spin round. He found himself facing the luxuriantly moustached stranger who had just come out from the shade of the trees.

Harold found it difficult to know what to say. This little man must have almost certainly overheard what he had just said.

Harold, at a loss, said somewhat ridiculously:

"Oh—er—good afternoon."

In perfect English the other replied:

"But for you, I fear, it is not a good afternoon?"

"Well—er—I—" Harold was in difficulties again.

The little man said:

"You are, I think, in trouble, Monsieur? Can I be of any assistance to you?"

"Oh no thanks, no thanks! Just blowing off steam, you know."

The other said gently:

"But I think, you know, that I could help you. I am correct, am I not, in connecting your troubles with two ladies who were sitting on the terrace just now?"

Harold stared at him.

"Do you know anything about them?" He added: "Who are you, anyway?"

As though confessing to royal birth the little man said modestly:

"I am Hercule Poirot. Shall we walk a little way into the wood and you shall tell me your story? As I say, I think I can aid you."

To this day, Harold is not quite certain what made him suddenly pour out the whole story to a man to whom he had only spoken a few minutes before. Perhaps it was overstrain. Anyway, it happened. He told Hercule Poirot the whole story.

The latter listened in silence. Once or twice he nodded his head gravely. When Harold came to a stop the other spoke dreamily.

"The Stymphalean Birds, with iron beaks, who feed on human flesh and who dwell by the Stymphalean Lake . . . Yes, it accords very well."

"I beg your pardon," said Harold staring.

Perhaps, he thought, this curious-looking little man was mad!

Hercule Poirot smiled.

"I reflect, that is all. I have my own way of looking at things, you understand. Now as to this business of yours. You are very unpleasantly placed."

Harold said impatiently:

"I don't need you to tell me that!"

Hercule Poirot went on:

"It is a serious business, blackmail. These harpies will force you to pay—and pay—and pay again! And if you defy them, well, what happens?"

Harold said bitterly:

"The whole thing comes out. My career's ruined, and a wretched girl who's never done anyone any harm will be put through hell, and God knows what the end of it all will be!"

"Therefore," said Hercule Poirot, "something must be done!"

Harold said baldly: "What?"

Hercule Poirot leaned back, half-closing his eyes. He said (and again a doubt about his sanity crossed Harold's mind):

"It is the moment for the castanets of bronze."

Harold said:

"Are you quite mad?"

The other shook his head. He said:

"Mais non! I strive only to follow the example of my great predecessor, Hercules. Have a few hours' patience, my friend. By tomorrow I may be able to deliver you from your persecutors."

IX

Harold Waring came down the following morning to find Hercule Poirot sitting alone on the terrace. In spite of himself Harold had been impressed by Hercule Poirot's promises.

He came up to him now and asked anxiously:

"Well?"

Hercule Poirot beamed upon him.

"It is well."

"What do you mean?"

"Everything has settled itself satisfactorily."

"But what has happened?"

Hercule Poirot replied dreamily:

"I have employed the castanets of bronze. Or, in modern parlance, I have caused metal wires to hum—in short I have employed the telegraph! Your Stymphalean Birds, Monsieur, have been removed to where they will be unable to exercise their ingenuity for some time to come."

"They were wanted by the police? They have been arrested?"

"Precisely."

Harold drew a deep breath.

"How marvellous! I never thought of that." He got up. "I must find Mrs. Rice and Elsie and tell them."

"They know."

"Oh good." Harold sat down again. "Tell me just what—"

He broke off.

Coming up the path from the lake were two figures with flapping cloaks and profiles like birds.

He exclaimed:

"I thought you said they had been taken away!"

Hercule Poirot followed his glance.

"Oh, those ladies? They are very harmless; Polish ladies of good family, as the porter told you. Their appearance is, perhaps, not very pleasing but that is all."

"But I don't understand!"

"No, you do not understand! It is the other ladies who were wanted by the police—the resourceful Mrs. Rice and the lachrymose

Mrs. Clayton! It is they who are well-known birds of prey. Those two, they make their living by blackmail, mon cher."

Harold had a sensation of the world spinning round him. He said faintly:

"But the man—the man who was killed?"

"No one was killed. There was no man!"

"But I saw him!"

"Oh no. The tall deep-voiced Mrs. Rice is a very successful male impersonator. It was she who played the part of the husband—without her grey wig and suitably made up for the part."

He leaned forward and tapped the other on the knee.

"You must not go through life being too credulous, my friend. The police of a country are not so easily bribed—they are probably not to be bribed at all—certainly not when it is a question of murder! These women trade on the average Englishman's ignorance of foreign languages. Because she speaks French or German, it is always this Mrs. Rice who interviews the manager and takes charge of the affair. The police arrive and go to her room, yes! But what actually passes? You do not know. Perhaps she says she has lost a brooch—something of that kind. Any excuse to arrange for the police to come so that you shall see them. For the rest, what actually happens? You wire for money, a lot of money, and you hand it over to Mrs. Rice who is in charge of all the negotiations! And that is that! But they are greedy, these birds of prey. They have seen that you have taken an unreasonable aversion to these two unfortunate Polish ladies. The ladies in question come and hold a perfectly innocent conversation with Mrs. Rice and she cannot resist repeating the game. She knows you cannot understand what is being said.

"So you will have to send for more money which Mrs. Rice will pretend to distribute to a fresh set of people."

Harold drew a deep breath. He said:

"And Elsie—Elsie?"

Hercule Poirot averted his eyes.

"She played her part very well. She always does. A most accomplished little actress. Everything is very pure—very innocent. She appeals, not to sex, but to chivalry."

Hercule Poirot added dreamily:

"That is always successful with Englishmen."

Harold Waring drew a deep breath. He said crisply:

"I'm going to set to work and learn every European language there is! Nobody's going to make a fool of me a second time!"

www.ingramcontent.com/pod-product-compliance
Lightning Source LLC
LaVergne TN
LVHW051538170726
843492LV00006B/1839